GW01091492

Praise for *Wal*

"*Warrior of Light* is a transfor
vivid story-telling transports u
awareness, and deeper insight.

Davidji
Author of *Secrets of Meditation*

"*Warrior of Light* is a must read. This glorious tale of Martial
Arts, Adventure and Self -Discovery is an instant classic! With
over 30 years as a martial artist, Adam Brady brings to life
ancient martial arts philosophy and shares the Warrior's Way
through a brilliantly written story that inspires as much as it
entertains. I highly recommend this book to anyone seeking to
look inside and find their own inner 'Warrior of Light'".

Sifu Harinder Singh Sabharwal
Founder of JKDAA and Action Strength

"Adam Brady has done a masterful job of outlining Bruce Lee's
philosophy of Jeet Kune Do. Many of Lee's most famous
quotes are subtly referenced within *Warrior of Light*. The
importance of a strong foundation, the quality and not quantity
of training, being adaptable to change, staying in the present
moment with an uncluttered mind, being able to avoid conflict
when possible, and not setting limits were all realized as the
main character 'discovered the cause of his own ignorance'
during his journey. Brady has skillfully interspersed Lee's
pearls of wisdom that most certainly can apply to the reader's
life, martial artist or not."

Dr. Kirk D. Weicht
Head Instructor, Dallas-Fort Worth Jeet Kune Do Academy

"Inspiring! Relatable! Moving! *Warrior of Light* is a powerfully poignant metaphor for our soul's quest for finding our inner truth. This brilliantly articulated story illustrates the journey of a tenacious young man who was willing to risk losing it all in order to break through and go beyond the limitations of his mind and what society deems 'the norm' in order to truly find himself. This is my story, this is your story, and this is the story of anyone who is waking up as a conscious being. A must-read for anyone daring to embark on their own journey to greater self-awareness and higher ways of thinking, being and doing."

Tris Thorp
Vedic Master Educator and Internationally Recognized
Leader in the field of Emotional Integration

"Adam Brady is an expert in meditation, higher consciousness, and inner transformation. His wisdom is evident in this book as he guides readers to a new plateau of transcendence to achieve their true potential using martial arts as the backdrop. Get ready to be inspired as you embark on a journey of self-awareness."

Amanda Ringnalda
VP of Client Services & Operations at the Chopra Center
for Wellbeing and Vedic Master Educator

"As a martial artist, as someone who has followed one of the world's traditions of enlightenment, but more importantly as someone who has done both as a way of dealing with loss, I was impacted by Adam Brady's *Warrior of Light*. Kaladin's journey was my own, and that, more than the well-scripted fight scenes was what kept me moving through this novel. Adam Brady has captured something about both the martial arts and Zen that many try to express, but ultimately fail to do."

JB Jaeger
Dharma Teacher

"Adam Brady captures the true spirit of the Warrior in his epic story, *Warrior of Light*. Adam does an incredible job vividly choreographing martial arts techniques and scenes, and relating them to deeper spiritual practices. He integrates the fine martial arts with the practices of meditation and present moment awareness in a way that makes it easy for the reader to grasp. While the principles contained in this book apply to martial arts, the implications are far reaching and can be extrapolated into our everyday challenges. This story can serve as a powerful reminder to everyone that we must all be spiritual warriors and live our lives from that perspective. Adam Brady is a talented, insightful, gifted, courageous author and spiritual warrior. This book is a definite must read and may take a few readings to fully absorb all the concentrated messages within. I can't say enough about it! Phenomenal book!"

Sujata B. Patel
Owner, Wellness with Sujata
Certified Meditation and Yoga Instructor

"Adam Brady's first novel is an inspiring tale of true warrior wisdom. With elegance and grace he takes you, the reader, on a hero's journey that leaves you excited to move toward your own spiritual path and to stay to true to your heart just as Kaladin does. This is a heartwarming and welcome read for anyone searching to break down their own limitations, to move past their own perceptions of what is possible, and to courageously create a world of their choosing. And a must read for martial artists!"

Laura Giancarlo
Veteran Educator
Teen Leadership Facilitator
Martial Arts Practitioner and Instructor

"I was honored to meet Adam and I am even more honored to recommend you read *Warrior of Light*. A truly wonderful story."

Dr. Rodney Dunetz, AP
Certified Meditation and Yoga Instructor

"A beautifully written narrative of the warrior Kaladin, who after a deep personal loss is on a quest for self-discovery and a new way of life. Though based on a character proficient in the martial arts, this is a story that touches us all. Adam Brady is an exceptional master and teacher, and his book will bring something to everyone who reads it. Highly recommended."

Marisa Bourtin
Chopra Center Vedic Master

Warrior of Light

Cover design by Stephen Nauman
Author photograph by LRFerris Photography, LLC

Visit www. createspace.com to order additional copies.

ADAM BRADY

WARRIOR OF LIGHT

A FABLE

Warrior of Light

For Aidan, who is still young enough to have not forgotten that his possibilities are limitless

PROLOGUE

It was sunrise in Thelius. The first beams of light shone through the thick mountain mist that blanketed the ancient cobblestone streets. The buildings, steady as mountains themselves, were once part of a mighty fortress that guarded the city generations ago. Now they had become homes for the city's many inhabitants. Thousands lived there, within the mighty walls that had held off scores of invaders, conquerors and thieves. Since no one remembered how much time had passed since those days, the city's legacy had become more a matter of mythology than of historical fact.

But the people who lived there kept that mythical past very much alive. They, like their ancestors, were warriors, and proud warriors at that. Although there had been no enemy to fight for countless ages, they knew no other way to live. So, wanting to preserve their tradition and way of life, the men and women of Thelius would fight each other in nightly competitions. They trained endlessly, preparing for the next fight, the next chance to prove their strength and superiority. This was their way; a code all had grown to accept.

Thelius was the capital of Arkana, a vast country tucked against mighty mountains and stretching for hundreds of miles. Generations ago, the Arkanians had been a simple and peaceful people. When a horde of barbarians from the west invaded the land, however, the inhabitants of Arkana were forced to fight for their survival. Farming tools became swords and bows; tunics and robes were traded for armor and shields used by the brave Arkanian warriors.

These warriors fought inspired battles with the courage and dedication of a people whose very lives were at stake. Fighting in a war lasting 100 years, the men and women of Arkana not only defended their homeland, but also pushed back the invaders, and after countless campaigns and battles, finally defeated their enemy completely.

In the aftermath of this long and difficult war, the surviving barbarians were captured for a life of slavery. Arkana's frontier expanded to include the land of their enemy, doubling its size.

Thelius, the military stronghold of Arkana, became the capital of a now growing empire. Far from the peaceful hermitage it had once been, Thelius had become an enormous walled fortress, and along with the entire country, bore little resemblance to its former incarnation. Strength and power, qualities revered in combat, alongside with tradition, became the battle cry of a civilization forever changed by warfare.

This morning, as usual, the city's population was up and about to begin its training and sparring sessions.

The Arkanian fighting method was a hard and linear striking style of structured punches, kicks and blocking movements. It was a formal style in the sense that it was a rigid performance of techniques with fixed rules and boundaries. Arkanians would rise en masse to practice, or, more appropriately, *rehearse* the movements and patterns of combat they had known all their lives. This style of combat had become, quite literally, the state religion and its practice was a matter of personal duty.

The fighting forms had been handed down through countless generations of teachers and students. Victorious warriors from the battlefield were made to instruct the younger students in the techniques and strategies that had served them in battle. Movements and tactics, use of weapons, punches and kicks, all were performed as they had been used to defeat the enemy. Like a frozen moment in time, each pattern was preserved, repeated and passed down to the next generation for thousands of years.

In a small training hall on the outskirts of town, a veteran instructor addressed his students: "I will now teach you the *Kulika Form*. These techniques served our ancestors well in battle. Practice them often, so you too might use them in the Arena someday and bring honor to the memory of the great warrior Kulika." The instructor pointed to one of dozens of sculptures lining a raised shrine behind where he stood.

"To Kulika and Arkana we bring honor by training to fight as he did," the instructor said in a somber tone.

The children bowed their heads and chanted in unison, "The greatest honor is to uphold the tradition of Arkana!"

The boys and girls in the training hall watched as their instructor, wearing tan robes, lunged forward with a punch in the air that made his uniform "pop" from the force of the blow. Next came a kick, a back-fist strike, a double kick, a low block and the finishing movement, a palm strike.

"Ka-Yey!" the instructor shouted.

Throughout Thelius, the scene was repeated as instructors led their students through time-honored patterns of combat. All in the city knew these movements and training patterns. From the time children were able to walk, indeed, they had known little else. The city's Council had decreed that everyone must practice the style to protect the warrior tradition because without it, they were nothing. These fighting people never questioned the laws of the city, and they practiced endlessly for the chance to prove their skills in combat.

But over the years the training had become empty, the tradition hollow. The nightly battles had become little more than pit-fights during which the most base and primitive biological responses were displayed with cunning savagery. Normally, the evening fights could go on for up to an hour as the warriors followed strict rules of engagement. The fights often were not a matter of skill but one of endurance, in which both the lives and the pride of the warriors doing battle were put to the test.

In another part of the city, young men gathered in a training pavilion, not to practice a pattern of movements, but instead to spar in a full-contact training session.

Two bare-chested combatants, covered with sweat, had just finished a brutal round of sparring. They rested, near exhaustion, on the wooden rail of the training ring while elder instructors offered suggestions and criticism. One of the men was nursing a bloody lip, while the other was having difficulty standing on his right leg.

As the second round began, the two men assumed their fighting stances and moved toward each other. The man with the wounded leg was having trouble, something his opponent took advantage of by sweeping him off his feet with a low kick to his right leg. Coming in for the finishing blow, the dominating warrior delivered a solid punch to the midsection of the prone fighter. The victim doubled in pain as his rib cracked under the pressure of the strike.

It was a fierce and dangerous way of life; however, it was the driving ambition of all Arkanians to preserve their warrior tradition, even at the cost of life and limb.

In the Central Arena, where the battles were fought, combatants would frequently be beaten, maimed and even killed during a fight. This was accepted as part of the warrior's code and tradition. In fact, it was the most honorable way to die. All of city life was tied into this fighting tradition. Monuments and statues of great warriors, along with relics and implements of battle, lined the streets of the Arkanian capital. Even the bedtime stories of children were tales of the battles of long ago.

To fight meant status and respect. If one was unable to do battle, he was relegated to the menial tasks of civil service and city maintenance, only one step above the slave descendants of the barbarians captured in ages past.

Fighting was the life of a warrior. No one knew of any other way, except, perhaps one.

PART I

CHAPTER 1

Kaladin Lux had been up for nearly two hours when he decided to take a break from his empty-hand training. He sipped some tea as he stepped out onto his balcony to watch the action in the courtyard below. About 20 people were practicing an old combat form. They moved in unison, striking, blocking and shouting at their invisible foe. This was merely the warm-up. Next would come various drills, punching bag training and, finally, sparring.

Kaladin knew it all too well. Once, he had been part of a group like that, training day in, day out, over and over. That had been another time though, in what seemed like another life to him.

As his mind drifted into the past, Kaladin remembered how, seven months earlier, he had watched helplessly as his best friend Juna was slain without mercy in the Combat Arena. Juna's life had been taken by a vicious warrior named Valec, a zealot of the Arkanian warrior tradition if ever there was one. Valec had broken Juna's back in a brutal shoulder throw to the floor of the arena.

Juna, like all of the warriors who stepped into the ring, understood the danger, but despite his devotion to his fighting style, had not expected to die for it. His fight was only to last until he or Valec could no longer continue the combat. However, Juna's skill and tenacity had sent Valec into an uncontrollable rage that resulted in the final blow. Although the force Valec used in his technique was unnecessary, he followed the structured rules of engagement. This pleased the city's Council of Elders who judged the fight and found him without guilt.

The sights and sounds of that night hung heavy in Kaladin's mind: the thick air in the Arena, the howling crowd, the final and gruesome sound of breaking bones. Details he tried desperately to forget haunted his days and made for more than a few sleepless nights.

Kaladin was forever changed that night. Not only did he lose his childhood friend of 28 years, but he had seen how Arkanian tradition literally condoned an act of brutal violence that robbed another human being of his life. He knew something was terribly wrong when people could justify, even glorify, barbaric and savage behavior in the name of past history and tradition.

Now Kaladin had begun to question, to reflect on both his mortality and his way of life for the first time. *Why does it have to be this way? Why must we hurt each other to preserve our history? Can't we rise above the hostility and violence we've learned to live by? Isn't there more than this...?* Thoughts such as these would often consume Kaladin's mind in the months that had passed since Juna's death.

Most of the people in the city trained in large groups to maintain the continuity and purity of their style, or so Kaladin was told. But Kaladin had chosen to keep to himself these days. It could be risky to go against the status quo of the Arkanian traditions, yet he was looking for something new, something different, even though he wasn't certain what it was. Kaladin felt that whatever he was seeking could only be found by departing from the way things had always been. It was a risk worth taking.

This move to break away from his family training group and practice alone following Juna's death was a decision that troubled Kaladin's parents.

"It's not right for you to be on your own so much, son," his father had told him one evening. "You belong with your family and with what you've always known. That will help you move past Juna's death."

"I just need more time," Kaladin had replied.

"You know that I am friends with several members of the Council of Elders and that they are not fond of those who train in solitude. Return to our family training group before they become suspicious."

"I promise, when I feel ready, I'll come back."

Kaladin had no desire to go back, though. During his solitude his spirit had begun to flourish. A deep and powerful longing to know the truth about himself and the way he was living his life was slowly replacing Kaladin's grief over the loss of his friend. The sadness was still there, but instead of being consumed by it, he used it as fuel for the many questions he was facing.

Blowing across the lip of his teacup, Kaladin thought back to his first day out on his own. There, in that empty field months ago, he had dared to experiment, to step into the unknown. This was not the routine exercise he and Juna had rehearsed as boys. This was an exploration of what he was capable of, and he relished the sheer joy of it.

He remembered how he had broken individual techniques out of their combat pattern to study the transition between movements. Then he rearranged the order of the techniques to see how quickly his mind could adapt to the new pattern. Doing so, he found his mind became more flexible, dynamic, and capable of adapting to an opponent's movements. Time flew by that day as he trained, so great was his excitement from the rediscovery of his own abilities.

But later that evening as Kaladin walked home through the dimly lit streets, he heard the roar of the crowd from the Arena in the city center and his mind was flooded with images from the horrible night his friend was killed. He struggled to understand how Valec had been able to overwhelm Juna as he had.

Kaladin tried to analyze the fight, to see where it went wrong and how he might have fought differently. Yet what stuck in his mind was the rage, the anger that fueled Valec's onslaught. The thought unsettled Kaladin and he realized that this may be a key to his understanding, but the answer was elusive, deeply hidden by his own sense of loss.

Despite this emotional frustration, Kaladin had continued to focus on his training, pushing himself to be the best he could be. Putting aside the old patterns and forms, Kaladin began to explore the nature of his fighting style.

In the evenings while the population of Thelius was cheering in the Arena, Kaladin would study ancient books of combat, martial art and history that were kept in the city's old library. Rarely were the books opened; rather they were kept as trophies and artifacts to support the old legends.

This new knowledge inspired Kaladin to rethink the ideas about combat that he had grown to accept. Like a scientist, he analyzed the old limiting movements that had prevented his style from being a truly *living* form of effective and efficient combat. He was beginning to understand what was extraneous and unnecessary in the way he had learned to fight.

He replaced the traditional and repetitive training of his youth with exercises and drills to enhance his speed, power, reflexes and timing. Some of these practices he learned from the old texts, while others he adapted and experimented with to suit his own needs, something he knew the Council of Elders would *never* condone.

This striving for excellence led him to the realization that many of the limits he once thought were insurmountable were in fact simply old beliefs that he could change, and in changing his beliefs, he was starting to change himself.

Remembering these things made Kaladin pause as he drank his tea. "All the more reason to train alone," he thought aloud as he watched the mechanical movements of the students in the courtyard. "Best to wait until I'm able to show them what I've learned. Then they'll see that there is another way."

"No, not like that," shouted a voice from the courtyard.

Kaladin looked closer and saw an instructor lecturing a student on her punching form. "You mustn't turn your hand that way or your technique will have no speed and your opponent will be able to block the punch."

Kaladin rolled his eyes. *The position of her hand has nothing to do with how fast the punch will be*, Kaladin thought to himself.

He recalled how once he accepted that speed was simply a matter of how fast he could move his muscles. However, he recently had started to realize that his mind played a more vital part in the performance of a technique than his bones and muscles. Kaladin was learning that changing what he *believed* affected his ability to fight better, and presented staggering possibilities for what he could become both as a warrior and as a human being.

He swirled the tea in his cup gently while watching the group class begin their training pattern for what seemed like the 100th time.

The volume of the training is **not** *proportionate to the quality. It's not about training harder,* he thought. *It's about training smarter!*

And train smarter Kaladin had. He had found ways to eliminate unnecessary movements, he had discovered the ability to flow seamlessly from one technique to the next, and he had grasped more direct and effective methods of attack. Transcending the boundaries of speed, timing, body mechanics, power and coordination that he had formerly believed were written in stone had become his passion in the time since Juna's death. He knew he had made progress during this time on his own, but he had yet to know just how good he had become.

Finishing the last of his tea, Kaladin stepped back inside his dwelling to resume training. With so many different aspects of the martial arts one could focus on, Kaladin had learned to follow his instincts, since they always knew which areas needed the most work. Today's workout had been centered on rhythm and coordination. Through careful focus on his punches, kicks and hand traps, Kaladin found he could launch attacks with several limbs at virtually the same time. In the past, a punch was followed by a block, then a kick, then another punch, a kick and a block, in a very structured, choppy rhythm. However, Kaladin's training had produced something altogether different. Unlike the one-for-one trading of blows, this sequence of movements produced a broken rhythm and delivered three strikes in the time it used to make one.

Now, if only I can coordinate it all a little tighter, he thought as he threw a whirlwind combination of blows at his training dummy.

"Owww!" Kaladin reeled back in pain as the tip of his elbow slammed into the arm of the dummy. He winced and shook off the throbbing in his elbow, wishing his wooden opponent could tell him what he was doing wrong. With three rough-hewn wooden arms protruding from its trunk-like base, the dummy seemed to be mocking Kaladin in his pain. All morning he had been having the same problem, and he was beginning to grow frustrated. Trying to deliver the "perfect" attack was all he could think about now.

He tried again, only to suffer the same result. Recoiling in anger, Kaladin bit his lip and exhaled forcefully, the only thing keeping him from cursing aloud. *If only Juna were here, he could tell me what I was doing wrong*, he thought.

Kaladin fondly recalled how they used to train together, spotting each other's technique while providing criticism, advice and encouragement. He deeply wished for those days to return and for Juna to be able to share in his newfound excitement and passion for training. But Kaladin cut his thoughts short when he remembered why he was training alone and what had brought him to this moment. *Juna can't help you anymore Kaladin*, he said to himself. *He's not here. It's up to you now.*

Kaladin tightened the ponytail that held his sandy blond hair in place, closed his eyes and took a long deep breath. The pain in his elbow began to fade and he started to let go of the attachment he had felt so strongly for the perfect technique. His mind went blank for a moment, and then, slowly, a picture of himself began to form in his mind's eye, standing ready to launch into his attack. He watched vividly, seeing himself bursting forward in a blur of speed, delivering the perfect combination of strikes in a fraction of a second.

The image faded into a mental void as Kaladin's blue eyes opened wide and his body shot forward into the attack he had watched in his mind moments before. *Diggita-diggita-crack!* He struck the dummy with such speed and force that the wooden brace holding it up folded in two under the pressure. Pieces of the dummy tumbled to the floor with a thud as Kaladin stared in disbelief. "Wha...What?," he stammered to himself. "Where did that come from?"

He was stunned, but elated at the same time. *What a breakthrough!* No one had ever delivered strikes like that... until now. *Everyone will be amazed when they see what is possible*, thought Kaladin.

CHAPTER 2

Peeking through the window, the setting sun washed the room in a soft crimson light. Kaladin moved across the floor, twirling his combat sticks in a wide figure-eight pattern. Like some kind of tribal dance, the shadows on the wall mimicked his movements with perfect timing.

Kaladin had spent the afternoon experimenting with his footwork and had chosen to adopt a more dynamic stance. In doing so he found that he could greatly improve his mobility and economy of motion. Up on his toes, he could move in and out of the range of an opponent's attack with far more ease than if he used the stances of his old style. Like the fixed poses of statues, the old stances had structure and stability, but no flexibility or ease of movement. The large and demonstrative motions he had learned as a boy had no place in this new way of fighting.

Combat is about movement, Kaladin thought as he improvised and readjusted his footwork. His shadow-sparring took on a life of its own as he danced around the room, his sticks a blur of motion.

Time had passed quickly for Kaladin as he continued to explore his newfound style of fighting. The night of Juna's death had planted the seed of a new vision in Kaladin's mind. That seed had been nourished by research, creativity and innovation as Kaladin continued to redefine what it meant to be a warrior.

Suddenly, from out of nowhere, Kaladin was struck by an unexpected revelation: *If I were to eliminate all of the unnecessary movement during a fight, it would cut the length of a battle in half!* This idea was unheard of, and Kaladin was shocked by its implications.

"If the goal isn't to perform, but *to overcome the opponent*, then even the rules of engagement are just boundaries that prevent the evolution of our style," he said out loud to himself.

Deep within, Kaladin hoped for the chance to share these insights and teach others how they too could overcome their restrictions. It had become a growing concern for him, not only because he so wanted to share this new knowledge, but also because he knew the more he rejected the Arkanian tradition, the greater the risk of punishment if he failed to convince his fellow warriors.

A knock at the door interrupted Kaladin's training. Living in a small lodging tucked away in a quiet part of the city, he had few visitors during his reclusive solitude. He wondered who it could be as he put away his equipment and walked to the door.

It was his brother Banno. Kaladin greeted him warmly and invited him inside. They exchanged a few pleasantries before Banno got to the point of his visit: he had been sent by their father to see why Kaladin hadn't yet returned to training in the family's local group.

"I'm sorry, Banno. It's just that I feel I have so much to learn these days. I don't want to spend my life rehearsing the same old fighting traditions when I feel there is so much beyond them."

"That tradition is what made our family, Kal. Remember that," Banno replied. "We were born of out of tradition, and we should all be willing to die for it. And ignoring our way of life is only asking for trouble."

Kaladin thought hard about his brother's words. His family had indeed come from the highest levels of the warrior tradition. His father, who had been, and still was, a formidable opponent, would probably be asked to occupy a seat on the Council of Elders soon. Kaladin's mother was also a strong warrior in her own right. Perhaps he should consider trying things the old way again, just for a little while.

"I will try, Banno." he said reluctantly. "But ever since Juna died, something's changed".

"Come train with us. We'll help you change it back," Banno replied.

Staring into the candle flame on his bedside table that night, Kaladin thought about what his brother had said and decided to return to his family's training group the next day. Perhaps he could modify his skills to fit into the old patterns he had known as a child and thus show his family all he had learned.

That next morning Kaladin was training with his family, just like when he was a child. But as he practiced the ancient fighting patterns and forms, he began to feel a constriction in his body and mind. He began to daydream as he rehearsed the empty patterns. His mind drifted back to the first time he had properly performed a sidekick and how proud his parents were that day. If only they would be as excited about the progress he had made over these last few months. He did love his family and he wanted to make them happy, but he just didn't feel as if he belonged there anymore.

When the morning training was finished, Kaladin excused himself by explaining that he still wasn't ready to resume his training with them. Although visibly dismayed, his parents nodded and tried to accept their son's decision.

"You're always welcome, Kal," his mother said as he turned to go. "Don't stay away too long."

"I know, Mother. I hope you can be patient with me. I've just had a lot on my mind since Juna died."

"That was over seven months ago, son!" his father said. "You can't grieve forever. You know Juna wouldn't want that. He'd want you to go on, to honor what he fought for."

"It's not just Juna," Kaladin said. "There are just some things I need to sort out for myself."

"We'll be here when you do," his mother replied, as only a mother could.

As Kaladin headed out the front gate of his family home he turned and waved goodbye to his parents.

"He worries me," his father whispered.

"Me too," replied his wife. "Me too."

Walking home alone in the morning sunshine, Kaladin was nearly overcome with emotion. The love of his family meant so much to him, but he didn't know how he could ever show them all he was learning without risking their rejection. Sadly, he knew that the path he was following was one he had to travel alone for now. Perhaps in time he could share his knowledge, but it was not yet that time. He hoped his family would understand.

Later that night, Kaladin was off on his own again experimenting with body-movement drills. He focused intently upon his exercises so not to let his thoughts drift back to the morning training with his family. As he slowly performed strikes with total presence of mind on his muscles and the movements of his body, Kaladin was able to feel the most natural and fluid expression of the technique. When he then performed the motion at normal speed, it flowed as if it were being spontaneously created for the first time, rather than being performed for the hundredth. *This is how training is meant to be*, he thought, wishing the others could grasp its implications.

Kaladin didn't sleep well that night and woke the next morning with a restless and agitated mind. He felt overwhelmed and confused by his thoughts and feelings and struggled not to think about them as he ate breakfast. It seemed to be no use, though. "I can't train like this, not in this state of mind," he said to himself, and decided to go for a walk through the city.

He strolled slowly without direction, his mind flooded with thoughts of his family, the insights he had gained, his desire to share his knowledge, and the uncertainty that seemed to surround him. He walked out beyond the gates and into the nearby hills, barely noticing his surroundings, having become so lost in thought. The more he tried to find peace, the more elusive it became. Turbulent thoughts were strung together like pearls on a necklace, seemingly without end.

On the verge of a mental breakdown, Kaladin slumped down against the trunk of an ancient tree.

Ahhhhggg! Kaladin grimaced as he felt the last of his strength fade away. *I won't be able to show anyone anything if I can't stop all this noise in my head,* he thought. He sighed deeply, feeling totally lost.

Inhaling long and deep, Kaladin closed his eyes and let the fresh air fill his lungs. He paused and noticed that in that moment his thoughts seemed to still themselves slightly. He breathed again, watching his breath with more attention and noticed that all of his worries and frustrations were slowly beginning to let go and fade into the background. Unexpectedly, a sparkle of insight crept into Kaladin's consciousness…in the simple act of taking a breath, could he have discovered the peace of mind he had been struggling so hard to find?

He breathed again, slowly watching his breath rise and fall, feeling the air fill his lungs, noticing it all. Kaladin gradually began to lose himself in his breath, in and out, over and over. He became aware as his thoughts drifted to his family, or to Juna's death, but coming back to his breath, the serenity and stillness would return.

Kaladin's relief was immense. His body relaxed and tension began to dissolve. He felt free…

When he opened his eyes, perhaps 30 minutes later, the world looked different somehow. He wasn't sure *what* was different, but he could feel that something had changed. With clarity of mind he hadn't known before, Kaladin rose, knowing he would be able to continue his training and study.

This new mental discipline became part of Kaladin's training practice. Morning workouts now began with a period of breathing meditation in addition to the physical training of his body. Stilling the restless inner chatter that had held him captive day in and out allowed his awareness to expand and his insight to grow. The silence he experienced infused his daily activity, allowing him to act without the stress of thoughts and judgments. He could simply *be* as he flowed effortlessly from one technique to the next.

Three weeks later, while practicing his meditation, an idea suddenly filled him with a flash of inspiration: *You are not here to overcome your opponent. You are here to overcome yourself.*

In that instant, Kaladin realized that being a true warrior meant not mastering the body, but mastering the mind. He was filled with excitement as he left his quiet hilltop and headed back toward town. He knew this was the inspiration he had been waiting for. Now he was ready to share what he had learned. Surely the people of Thelius could not ignore such important insights. Unheard of as it was, such knowledge was far too important not to share.

As he neared the Arena, he noticed a crowd had formed around the billboard. He knew it meant that the fighting roster had been posted for the week; people were eager to see whom they would face in battle. Kaladin's interest in the fights waned as he had grown and developed, but for some odd reason, he felt compelled to check the roster today.

To his surprise, as he read through the list he found himself scheduled to fight. And not only that, he was to fight Randak, Valec's younger brother, in a challenge match! Kaladin was stunned. He hadn't requested to be put back into combat rotation, yet there his name was.

"How…?" he mused out loud.

He felt a hand on his shoulder. "Your father thought it was time for you to defend your family's tradition again, Kaladin." It was Pyral, one of the city elders. "You can't run from who you are."

I wasn't running, just waiting, Kaladin thought as he nodded reluctantly. He knew he had no choice in the matter. In seven days' time he would have to fight.

Well, I wanted a chance to show them what I've learned, he thought as he walked toward home. *This must be the time.* The more he thought it over, surprise and concern gave way to excitement and anticipation. He could demonstrate the freedom he had discovered and show everyone how they too could be free. Although he had no desire to fight Randak, he knew that this fight was the best way to bring his insights out into the open.

CHAPTER 3

The next week seemed to pass like an eternity for Kaladin as he anticipated the fight. It wasn't the act of fighting that he looked forward to as much as the thought of sharing his newfound knowledge. He loved the idea of showing everyone how they could train for their own sake, experiencing the simple bliss of an integrated mind, body and spirit during combat. Perhaps they would give him a special honor, or place on the Council. Ah, but he was getting ahead of himself.

Kaladin knew that Randak would be a fierce opponent. He was larger and more powerful than Kaladin and would try to use that to his advantage. The differences in size weren't of concern, though. Kaladin knew raw strength and power should be a moot point when brought to bear upon his refined technique. There was no way to be sure until the fight, though.

It was this uncertainty and unpredictability that preoccupied Kaladin. He understood that anything could happen in the Arena and he knew a great deal was at risk. If he failed, he could be injured or killed and his message would go unheard. In addition, the act of publicly going against long-held beliefs and tradition was a dangerous proposition, but Kaladin knew it was now or never, and was willing to take the risk.

Finally the evening of the fight arrived, and Kaladin was as prepared as he could be. Despite what had happened the last time he was in the Arena, he was strangely calm as he dressed in his tan combat uniform. All his learning, everything he wished to share that night, seemed like a quiet snowfall in the background of his consciousness.

Once Kaladin passed through the large archway of the Arena, two guards escorted him to a small bench at one end of the great rectangular platform. For the moment, he was content to sit and wait for the Council and his opponent to arrive. He could almost feel the crowd's anticipation of the evening's fight. It was not an entirely pleasant feeling. These people expected bloodshed; it made little difference who won or lost.

The Arena itself seemed to echo the battles it had witnessed over the years. An ancient structure of unparalleled design and majesty, it was the focal point of Arkanian culture and tradition. Stone pillars lined the outer edges of the oval Arena, each topped with a statue of a great warrior. Inside the massive walls, thousands of spectators could fill its seats to witness the nightly matches. Through hundreds of years of combat, the Arena had nearly taken on a life of its own. A gruesome, violent and savage atmosphere reeked from the very stones themselves. In the flickering torchlight that illuminated the Arena, one could almost see the spectral warriors of antiquity as they fought each other in ghostly combat.

It didn't take long for the stands to fill and the Council of Elders to file into their private box, their gray robes signifying the highest level in warrior society. Randak had taken his place at the opposite end of the platform and was performing a combat form in preparation for the fight. Kaladin, however, sat in stillness and observed the thoughts of his mind slowing to a standstill. He knew what he had come to do and was clear about his intention. Now was the time.

The great bronze gong that signaled the beginning of the nightly fights resonated throughout the Arena. The crowd grew quiet as the combatants were introduced at either end of the platform. Each stood and bowed to the Council, then to each other. The presiding Council member motioned for Kaladin and Randak to take their places and stand on guard. This fight, like the battle between Juna and Valec, would go on until one or both of the warriors were unable to continue.

Time seemed to stand still for Kaladin as he waited for the signal to start. With a clear tone, the gong resounded throughout the Arena, breaking the silence and signaling the fight to begin.

Randak initiated the combat and rushed at Kaladin, but stopped short when he saw the non-traditional stance his adversary had adopted. Kaladin saw Randak's pause as an opening and took it, attacking his opponent's lead leg. The kick chopped into Randak's thigh, and he buckled in pain. As Kaladin danced out of reach, Randak stared at the spot where his leg had been hit and then at Kaladin.

He rushed Kaladin again, this time launching a punch to the face, but instead of blocking the punch, Kaladin targeted it with his elbow. The bones of Randak's hand cracked as Kaladin's elbow slammed into them full force.

Randak, staggered by the pain, cradled his hand as Kaladin rushed forward in a blinding blur of punches to the face that sounded like a drum roll. Stumbling backward, Randak tried to defend himself, but Kaladin grabbed him by the neck and pulled him in for a head-butt. The top of Kaladin's head drove solidly into his opponent's defenseless face. Randak toppled to the straw mat, unconscious. The fight was over.

In less than a minute Kaladin had totally defeated his opponent in what appeared to be a flawless expression of combat. The Arena had fallen dead silent. Then, slowly, a low murmur could be heard that began to grow louder and louder. The faces of the Council members were wide-eyed and white as ghosts as members of the audience looked at each other in surprise and disbelief.

Kaladin waited for a response and began to smirk, allowing his emotions to peek through. The emotions he felt weren't what he had expected, however. Although Kaladin's heart was still racing from the overwhelming counter-attack he had directed at Randak, the inner peace he had felt before the match was gone. In its place, he felt a growing defensive and hostile attitude that he found difficult to understand.

"I'll kill you!" shouted someone in the crowd. Kaladin looked up and saw Valec vaulting benches and spectators to get to the platform. He made it to the far end, where his brother lay in a heap. Kaladin focused on his new opponent, who was charging at him at full speed. Valec leaped into the air to deliver a deadly flying kick, but Kaladin had circled out of the way. Valec continued, attempting a kick to the head, a punch to the stomach, and a back-fist to the face, all of which Kaladin easily parried or sidestepped.

Kaladin hadn't expected this. He hadn't counted on fighting Valec, and why hadn't the Council stopped him? Valec had obviously overstepped his bounds. His brother had clearly lost to Kaladin's skill, not by any trick or deceit, and he would recover. Why did the Council not take action?

Valec continued his attack with a relentless series of punching and kicking combinations, all of which failed to connect with their finely-tuned target.

As Kaladin continued to dodge Valec's attacks though, he felt the hostility growing inside him. Thoughts flooded his mind like a torrent with every moment that passed. *How dare he attack me? I won the fight.* Hostility was turning into anger and anger into rage. *You! You killed my best friend! It was you!* Images of Juna's death and Valec standing over the lifeless body of his friend flashed through Kaladin's mind. With every swing and kick Valec made, the hatred boiled closer to the surface.

Unfortunately, Kaladin's thoughts became too much of a distraction and Valec's fist connected with a solid blow to his jaw. Kaladin reeled backward from the power of the blow, staggering to keep his balance.

Surprisingly, Valec paused for a moment in his attack. He looked at the Council members in their box and then back at Kaladin. He seemed to be waiting for Kaladin's response. All the while, the murmur bubbling through the crowd was growing louder. No one knew what would happen next.

Kaladin shook off the blow and looked up to see Valec smiling at him smugly. The punch had snapped him out of his reverie and brought his attention back to the moment. The pain was hardly noticeable to Kaladin, beneath the flood of his emotions. He glared at the Council out of the corner of his eye. If they weren't going to stop this madness, he would have to.

Kaladin drew a deep breath. He knew if his mind wasn't still he'd stand no chance against Valec. He took another breath and centered himself. *Use your emotions; don't let them use you.* The thought rang through Kaladin's mind like a bell. The words faded with each breath like a soft echo, growing softer and softer until all that remained was silence.

With a new resolve, Kaladin locked his eyes upon Valec, and returned to his fighting stance. Valec gave a sinister nod of approval toward Kaladin as he clenched his fists, causing the knuckles of his hands to crack.

Suddenly, Valec growled and threw a strong punch toward Kaladin's face. However, Kaladin's mind was clear now, and he saw the punch coming. Focused upon nothing short of the total destruction of his adversary, Kaladin parried the punch with his left hand while simultaneously punching deeply into Valec's attacking arm with his right. As his knuckles sank into muscle and nerve, Kaladin shot the fingers of his left hand into Valec's eyes and kicked sharply into his exposed shin. Valec's head rocked back from the jab into his eyes. He was unable to see Kaladin's back-fist as it connected heavily with his nose.

Kaladin continued by driving a knee into Valec's stomach, causing him to buckle over and expose his lead leg to another heavy kick that sank deep into the muscle.

A series of straight punches to the face followed, forcing Valec to backpedal away from the vicious assault. Unable to retreat in time, he raised his arm to block the attack. Kaladin, expecting this, simultaneously grabbed Valec's arm at the wrist, twisted his waist, and drove his forearm into the elbow joint of his attacker.

Valec's arm popped under the pressure and he gasped in pain. Kaladin continued without pause, though, slapping first to Valec's groin, and then again to his left ear. Finally, Kaladin leaned his weight into his forearm and gave a powerful shove into Valec's chest. Unable to maintain his balance, Valec sailed backwards and slid across the platform.

Bloodied and clutching his tingling arm, Valec struggled to return to his feet as Kaladin positioned himself just out of reach. Kaladin knew that with the injuries Valec had sustained, it would be foolish to continue the fight. However, Valec dragged himself up into a standing position, wiped the blood from his nose, and set his eyes upon Kaladin.

When Kaladin saw the difficulty with which Valec moved he looked long and deep into the eyes of his adversary and slowly shook his head from side to side. *No more.* He thought to himself. *Let it end here.* When Valec saw this, though, his eyes widened into a bloodthirsty rage and he rushed straight at Kaladin.

Valec swung wildly at Kaladin as their bodies slammed together into a clinch. At this distance though, his punches were too jammed to have any effect.

Kaladin turned his hip into Valec's side while reaching around to grasp his opponent's waist and with one deft movement, bent his body over, flipping Valec through the air.

Valec landed with a resounding thud that kicked up dust from the straw mat beneath him. Dazed from the fall, he tried desperately to get up. Unfortunately for him, Kaladin had mounted Valec's chest, pinning his back to the ground. From this position, Kaladin rained a series of unstoppable punches to Valec's head. Panicked and trapped, Valec squirmed to get back on his feet, but Kaladin's position held him firmly in place.

Kaladin knew Valec had no hope of escape and delivered blow after blow to his foe's defenseless face. He could feel his anger and resentment struggling to come to the surface once more, and he had little hope of controlling it now. All the anger, all the rage, all the hate he had felt boiling inside wanted to pour out with a vengeance. *Yessss! He deserves this. For killing Juna, he should pay!* The words slithered through Kaladin's mind like a serpent. They wrapped themselves around him, entangled him, as the moment became a blur of emotion. Shocked to hear himself think such thoughts, Kaladin paused in his onslaught. He sat on Valec's chest, one fist cocked next to his ear, primed to deliver a fatal blow, and waited.

With the last of his strength, Valec squirmed desperately and turned onto his stomach to avoid the unbearable pressure of Kaladin's forthcoming punch. Seeing this, Kaladin, with a softened resolve, grabbed a fistful of Valec's brown hair and tugged his head back enough to wrap an arm around his neck. In a few moments, Valec was unconscious next to his brother.

Kaladin climbed off the still body of his opponent and tried to compose himself. Although the fight was over, he was still in an unresolved state of emotional turmoil. All the hostility and anger he felt, where had it come from? Why couldn't he control it? His head spun in the aftermath as he looked around the now *very* still Arena.

"Enough," shouted the presiding Council member. "Kaladin Lux, son of Sona, stand and face the Council!" The force of the command took Kaladin aback, and he did as he was told.

The Council members whispered amongst themselves as a growing unrest spread through the crowd. *Shouldn't they be cheering?* thought Kaladin as he scanned the faces in the crowd. The fight had gone much better than he ever could have anticipated, despite Valec's intrusion. His movements had been fast and smooth, his technique virtually without flaw. Yet the crowd wasn't impressed. Something was very wrong.

"Kaladin Lux," the voice of the elder repeated, "What gives you the right to disgrace our tradition and heritage?"

Disgrace? Was he serious? Kaladin had proven that the limitations of tradition prevented people from experiencing the freedom of unlimited combat. He was showing people how to build a stronger tradition, a nobler heritage for the future, a better way of fighting.

"I meant *no* offense to the Council, your honor," Kaladin stammered. "I was only trying to show what I had learned."

Kaladin was still not thinking clearly in the wake of the fight.

"Learned indeed," another Council member growled in a scathing tone. "Your so-called learning has brought shame to our tradition and way of life."

"But I wanted you to see how much more we have to learn," Kaladin insisted. "Self-protection and self-perfection go hand in hand."

"Nonsense!" The elder glared at him. "We fight *to* fight, not to reinvent our way of life."

"But your honor, please, this knowledge is too important to ignore." The fog of emotion had begun to lift from Kaladin's mind and he struggled to find a way to convince the Council of his good intentions.

"Indeed! Look at what this knowledge of yours wrought upon Randak and Valec!"

Kaladin looked unsympathetically toward the brothers, who were starting to regain consciousness. "But their injuries are mild compared to those that others have received in this very Arena!" Kaladin retorted. His thoughts drifted back to the time of Juna's death and how the Council dismissed Valec without punishment.

"Insolent boy!" the elder shouted. "The issue here is disrespect, not injury. Randak and Valec followed the dictates of our tradition. They fought within the rules of our style. You, on the other hand, saw fit to break these rules, using outlawed techniques, unorthodox movements and a haphazard style."

"Haphazard?" Kaladin was insulted. "Your honors, my movements looked chaotic only in light of the rigidity to which you have become so firmly bound."

This was the last straw, and Kaladin knew it. He didn't care, though. Like it or not, they had to know the truth.

"Silence!" There was more whispering amongst the Council. Finally, the presiding Council elder struck the gong to quiet the rumbling crowd. "Kaladin Lux, son of Sona, you have been charged with willfully breaking the rules of engagement and with the public disgrace of our style and tradition. How say you?"

Kaladin took a deep breath and paused.

"If striving to know my truest expression in combat, to understand the science of fighting and to share that knowledge with others is a crime, then I am guilty. To not express my nature as a warrior would be a far worse punishment than you could ever convey."

"We'll see about that," came the reply.

The crowd was on its feet now, booing and hissing at Kaladin. Randak and Valec had been helped off the platform and spear-wielding guards had taken up positions at either end of the ring.

Kaladin knew that the crowd could easily turn into a mob and mash him flat in an instant, but somehow the stillness he had been cultivating swept over him like a wave and he remained calm. The simple realization that the Council was not about to accept his point of view settled into his awareness, creating a stoic resolve. Kaladin was trying to hide his resentment toward the Council, but his feelings were difficult to deny. *Why can't you see it? What are you afraid of?* he thought to himself as the Council debated his punishment.

Time seemed to slow down and nearly stop for Kaladin again as he scanned through the angry crowd. He saw his family, hanging their heads in shame, all except his mother. She looked at him with a pained expression on her face, as if she knew she would never see him again.

"Kaladin Lux," the elder said slowly and deliberately, his temper cooling. "You are hereby banished from this city and the protection of its walls. You are never to return. Since you have chosen not to respect our way of life we will not allow you to be a part of it. Know also that it is only due to your family and father's reputation that the sentence of death has been overturned. Leave us that we may wash this night and your dishonor from our memory."

The elder signaled to the guards. They approached Kaladin, took him by the arms and escorted him from the platform, through the Arena, and out toward the street. Kaladin hardly heard the roaring of the crowd or the elder's voice as he urged everyone to forever forget what had just happened. Instead, Kaladin was strangely removed from it all, as if he were a spectator himself.

He watched in detachment as he was led to his dwelling to collect his few belongings. Feelings of anger, betrayal and finally sadness came and went as the guards led him through the city streets toward the outer gate. As the huge gates creaked open, he was marched past a line of hecklers, but numbness had overtaken him and their sneers and scowls had no effect.

Pausing for a moment, he noticed his family next to the gate. Kaladin took in the entire scene one last time. He looked into his mother's eyes, smiled softly and stepped through the gate with his bag of possessions slung firmly over his shoulder. He turned around when he heard the low groaning of the gates as they began to close. Watching the opening between them grow smaller and smaller, he stole one last look at his family before the cold "thud" of the wooden doors shut him out from the only world he had ever known.

PART II

CHAPTER 4

Kaladin walked along the rocky river bank with his bedroll slung loosely over his shoulder. The gentle gurgle of the water made a comforting sound as it cascaded over the odd-shaped stones protruding from its surface. Kaladin had been following the river south for several days. Not only was it more likely that he would find settlements along the river, but he would never lack food and water at the river's edge.

Over a month had passed since his exile. When he wasn't traveling, Kaladin had spent his days in training and meditation. He had continued to make progress as he trained, but whenever he thought of his failure to convince the Council to open their eyes to a new way of thinking, sadness and frustration overcame him. Sitting by his small fire under the stars each night, he would wonder what he might have done or said differently to make his message more acceptable.

But during the quieter moments of silence, he was coming to realize that he had done all he could. Not everyone was ready to accept his message. Knowing this gave Kaladin some comfort, and made him happy to be on his own. But at the same time he found himself missing his family and old way of life terribly. Knowing that they had always been there was a comfort he had taken for granted. Now with them gone, he felt a deepening sense of loss.

Pausing to sit along the river's edge one morning, Kaladin asked himself an unanswerable riddle: *Should I have remained safe and comfortable within the boundaries of tradition and not learn all that I have? Was it wise to break with the known and step out into a world of new and exciting possibilities, when the price of learning cost me everything I've known?*

He kicked the softly flowing water with the toe of his boot, gently stirring the muddy river bottom. The brown silt swirled briefly upstream before being washed away with the current. Seeing this, Kaladin rubbed his eyes and sighed. It didn't seem like going against the current could make much difference.

Hanging his head, Kaladin closed his eyes and ran his hands through his hair. He let go of his worries as best he could and lost himself in the sound of the river. Emptying his mind would soothe his emotional wounds more deeply than any amount of rational justification.

With the rolling water at his feet, Kaladin let the sound wash over him. Whispering softly in the back of his mind, memories of the fight and the stubborn resolve of the Council elders came and went. Like leaves on the flowing water, Kaladin watched the thoughts trickle through his mind. The most powerful image was the anger he had felt during the fight and his confrontation with the Council. The emotional turmoil of that night was unlike anything he had ever known and it troubled him greatly.

Fortunately, in his new wilderness home, it took effort to cling to the past. Opening his eyes, Kaladin saw beams of sunlight shining through the tall trees, heard the leaves dancing across the forest floor, and felt the cool mountain breeze as it whistled through the hillside.

Immersed in this natural beauty, Kaladin's city life began to feel remote, as if it had taken place a *lifetime* ago. Even in the short time he had been on his own he had learned a great deal, both about his rapidly evolving style of fighting and about himself. He didn't have to live or act according to someone else's rules; he could be whomever he chose.

Kaladin remembered how he used to be before Juna's death as he sat at the river's edge, bathed in the midday sun. He too once followed the rules and traditions of the Arkanian way of life, assuming it was the only way to live. He assumed it was the truth. He was a very different person now. He was different because he had *decided* to be different. Rather than making assumptions, Kaladin was seeking truth on his own, finding his own way.

Kaladin rummaged through the pebbles at his feet and tossed one into the water. The stone struck the surface, creating ripples that spread out over the smoothly flowing water. The ripples lapped up against the edge of the bank where Kaladin sat, and he was suddenly struck with insight. *It's all connected*, he thought to himself in wonder. *The stone makes the ripples, the ripples spread through the river, the river touches the bank, the riverbank touches the forest, and out into the world. Everything is different because of one stone.*

"And even though the stone is on the bottom, the ripples keep going," he thought aloud. The observation stunned him. If it were all bound together, then maybe there was a way to utilize the connection in combat. This idea seemed to be both a radical and abstract insight even for Kaladin, but something about it stuck with him, nevertheless. He gave the concept more thought as he kneeled and gazed into the still water, not exactly sure how to make sense of his revelation, but *feeling* that he was on to something.

Maybe I was like that pebble, he thought, *spreading invisible ripples throughout the Arena that night*. Kaladin realized that perhaps he had been expecting too much. Rather than attempting to convince anyone to change the way they fought, simply the act of making others *aware* of new possibilities might bring about a change.

After all, he thought, *just because I can't see the change doesn't mean it's not happening. The pebble might not seem to make a big difference, but little changes can add up over time. Eventually, one pebble might change the entire course of the river!* Noticing his reflection in the water beneath him, Kaladin smiled and mused aloud, "Perhaps…perhaps I made a difference after all."

CHAPTER 5

As the days stretched out behind him, Kaladin ventured deeper and deeper into the wilderness. Solitude had become his lone traveling companion. For the most part he was content, wandering and training on his own, but Kaladin often longed for a friendly face. It seemed like an eternity since he was banished from Thelius, and with each passing day, he felt his isolation growing.

Making his way through the dense underbrush that lined the water's edge, Kaladin tried to clear a path so as not to have to wade through the chilly river. There was no other way to continue downstream since a steep slope hugged the river's edge tightly. The branches from nearby trees were like an obstacle course. Moss-covered and damp from an early morning rainfall, negotiating the limbs was slippery and treacherous work. Kaladin had fallen twice already and he still had several hundred feet left to go before the hillside opened up into a clearing. Normally the journey wouldn't have been so difficult, but peace of mind had become illusive for Kaladin recently, and his frustration was compounding the task at hand.

Troubled over memories from his fight in the Arena, Kaladin was continually haunted by the emotional chaos he had experienced while fighting Valec. Unable to explain the reasons for his anger and uncontrollable rage, Kaladin assumed that with time he would come to see why he had lost control and perhaps understand how he could prevent it from happening again. As the days went by, however, Kaladin had more and more difficulty with his feelings. He was becoming irritable, inpatient and bitter with himself at times. Despite his realization of the interconnectedness of all things, Kaladin was feeling more separate than ever. Little things such as a change in the weather or making a fire became enormous irritations. He had been having trouble sleeping at night and he could feel his discontent growing stronger every day. Meditation, which he had relied upon for the peace and insight it brought him in the past, now seemed to create an even more agitated mental atmosphere, one in which confusion and frustration clouded his thinking like a thick haze.

Stepping widely to his right, Kaladin ducked under a large thorny branch. Unseen by him, though, one of the wooden needles caught on his tunic and dug into his skin.

"Oww!" Kaladin erupted, scowling down at his shoulder. He yanked the thorn free and held the pointy obstacle well away from his body as he stepped through the opening in the brush. Pausing, he pulled his tunic away from his shoulder and found a small scarlet streak an inch long. He shook his head in disgust and yanked his tunic back in place.

"Fine warrior I am," he said aloud. "Can't even win a fight with a bush!" He mocked himself in apathy, wishing desperately to get to the clearing so he could rest a while.

Taking a deep breath, Kaladin composed himself and looked upward toward the unmoving hillside. "If I have to choose between you and these thorns, I'll take you." The hillside loomed in silent defiance as Kaladin began to climb.

Despite the odds he was facing, Kaladin wouldn't let himself give up. Something within urged him forward, not only along the hillside, but also through his growing emotional turmoil. He held on to hope, believing the answers would make themselves known to him.

Thirty more minutes of ducking, climbing and nearly crawling his way through tangled vegetation and bumpy slopes passed without incident and it looked as if Kaladin had reached the opening to the long sought after clearing in the hillside. He stepped up onto a gnarled log of what was once a thick tree trunk and looked around. To his surprise, though, what appeared to be a clearing was in fact a sharp drop, a steep embankment that Kaladin had been unable to see as he had moved upwards and away from the river's edge.

"Arrr!" Kaladin snarled to himself. "I've just about *had it* with this today..." Noticing the embankment was dotted with scattered stones and trees, he sputtered, "Well, won't this be tricky."

In his anger, Kaladin grimaced and kicked a rotten branch protruding from the log on which he stood. The branch, not as rotten as it looked, bounced against Kaladin's foot, pushing him off balance. The slippery wood squeaked as Kaladin lost his footing and tumbled headlong down the embankment.

Rolling end over end, Kaladin somehow narrowly missed the stones and saplings covering the slope. Even so, it was a bumpy, pain-ridden ride that ended with Kaladin covered in dirt, leaves and scratches as he rolled to a stop at the base of the hill.

Kaladin flung his bedroll and shoulder pack to the ground beside him. "Whuff," Kaladin exclaimed. "That was fun," he said sarcastically, as he knelt with his hands upon his knees, exhausted.

An hour later, Kaladin had found a suitable place to set up camp. He sat in the quiet shadows as he began his meditation. A few scattered rays of light from the afternoon sun splashed across the glade in a mosaic of shadows. The large trees towered around the small clearing like the walls of an ancient temple, long forgotten. Thick moss covered the ground, providing a cushion on which Kaladin could relax and let his mind go inward. It had been a trying day and he needed the physical rest of his meditation as well as the peace of mind he hoped it would bring him.

This evening seemed particularly bleak as Kaladin sat in stillness, observing his breath come and go. A chilly breeze whispered through the glade and stirred the leaves at his feet. Ten minutes passed, then 20. The sun had begun to set behind the trees, leaving a reddish orange hue in the sky overhead. The minutes seemed to groan by as Kaladin sat in silence, struggling to let his mind go deeper into the space between his thoughts.

Although his body was relaxed, Kaladin's mind was a chaotic, swirling storm of activity. Thoughts poured in from every side, seemingly without direction or meaning. Each time, he would come back to his breath, but it would only be moments before another thought tore through his mind like an arrow shot from a bow. Finally, after what seemed like an eternity, the silence overcame the uproar in his mind and Kaladin found a measure of peace.

A deep calm swept over him as he breathed into the stillness. At last, Kaladin could see things clearly, as they were, without the limitations of language and spoken words. He could simply be.

In this unusually deep silence, Kaladin wondered if he could find the answers that had eluded him these last several months. *Where had the anger come from?* he thought softly to himself. The question was swallowed up in the tranquility of his mind, leaving no trace. *Why was I so filled with rage that night?* he asked again. His thought faded like the ringing of a bell echoing over a distant landscape.

However, the answers weren't forthcoming. Kaladin waited patiently in the silence until a strong breeze whistled through the branches overhead and roused him from his meditation. Opening his eyes and looking around, Kaladin smiled lightly, enjoying the change in perspective that meditation brought, but still deeply concerned about the questions he had.

Sighing deeply, he rose and began to gather wood for a fire in the evening twilight. It would be a chilly night.

.

CHAPTER 6

Kaladin tossed and turned restlessly as he tried to sleep. Wrapped up in a thin blanket next to his small campfire, he rolled over to see the stars overhead. Through the high canopy of trees above, he could make out a few of the familiar constellations he had been taught as a boy. Ulto the Swordsman, Baultian the Loyal and Graunco Slayer of Reynak, shone down from their celestial home, reminding Kaladin of the stories his father had told him as a boy; stories in which these noble warriors had been eulogized in the very sky itself for their acts of bravery and fighting skill.

Lying there on the forest floor, he looked back over the events that had brought him to this moment. Juna's death, his rejection of traditional training methods, the experience of meditation, the fight in the Arena, his banishment and ongoing exile; all these episodes apparently unfolding in sequence seemed to point to a greater plan at work, but a plan still hidden from view.

Finally, fatigue and exhaustion took over and Kaladin's eyes became heavy. The desire to understand the meaning of his life faded into nothingness as he fell into a deep sleep, and in that sleep he dreamed.

❧

Kaladin looked around. This was unlike any place he had ever been before and he realized he must be dreaming. Heavy shades of gray and black were everywhere he turned. Huge stone columns, thick brick walls and dark looming statues towered all around him. An unearthly mist clung low to the ground and swished around his feet when he walked. The air was filled with the odor of age and decay. Despite its foreign appearance, though, there was something strangely familiar about it all.

Suddenly Kaladin recognized his surroundings. He was in the Arena, or what seemed like the Arena. It was different now, haunted and ghostly; all its gruesome, fetid and hateful qualities brought to life. He could hear a low groan perpetually echoing through the air, vibrating through his bones.

As he began to see more clearly, he could make out shadows in the stands, but they didn't look like people. They were ghostly, gaunt skeletons, pale creatures staring blankly out into the Arena, mouths open, moaning out the ghastly chord that Kaladin heard.

In the center of the Arena were two men, fighting in a slow-motion exchange of blows. Then there was another pair of warriors, and another, until the entire Arena was filled with macabre battling combatants. Kaladin turned his head from the grim spectacle. As he did, the groans of the spectators faded and he was alone. The Arena was empty save for two men in the center.

One of the men was Valec. Grim and shadowy, like the warriors that had fought before, he squared off against his opponent. The other warrior was different, though. He wasn't a dark shadowy figure like the others; his features were clearer, more distinct and a soft glow shone from his body. It suddenly occurred to Kaladin that he was watching himself fight Valec on that fateful night many months ago.

The fight unfolded quickly, almost a blur to the eye as Kaladin watched from his unique and removed perspective. In a flash, the fight had reached its climax with Kaladin's dream-self mounted upon Valec's chest, ready to deliver the fatal blow. To his horror, Kaladin could see his dream counterpart transform, becoming more blurred, darker and then turning into a deep crimson shade. The moment froze in time as Kaladin watched in terror as his other self began to radiate a reddish-black glow. The groan of the crowd returned even louder now and sent chills up Kaladin's spine. Here before him were his rage and anger coming to life, poised to erupt.

In that hideous frozen instant, as Kaladin's shadow side pulled his fist a notch higher to strike, he paused and looked the dreaming Kaladin dead in the eye. Terrified, Kaladin jumped back, unprepared to be seen in this shadowy otherworld. Snarling, on top of his helpless prey, Kaladin's spectral self moved his lips and a dark evil sound filled the air.

"I am you; you are me." The words washed over Kaladin like poison. He shook and felt his breath catch in his chest.

This wasn't happening, not like this. This isn't the way it happened. Kaladin said to himself.

"This is how it should have happened," the shadow whispered back. He looked down once more to see his prey beneath him and bared his teeth.

"No!" Kaladin screamed and began to run toward his counterpart, but it was too late.

As Kaladin's otherworldly self delivered the fatal blow to Valec's chest, an incredible burst of energy enveloped both warriors in an enormous explosion. The shock wave threw Kaladin to the ground and bathed him in a blast of hot air. As he raised his head to glimpse the spot where the two warriors had been, all he could see was a deeply burned patch of earth. Stunned, his head fell back against the ground. The groaning of the crowd faded into silence and he closed his eyes.

Just as he thought he was about to wake from the nightmare, Kaladin heard a strange sound fill the air. Like a soft musical strain, the faint melody was a soothing combination of sounds blended together. A heartbeat, rolling waves, singing birds; they all flowed together into one amazing vibration.

Kaladin rolled over onto his side and felt the sandy gravel of the ground beneath his fingers. He could tell he was still in the Arena. Opening his eyes and rising to his feet, he saw the same dull gray outline as before but now it felt different. The grisly negativity that had haunted the walls seemed to have faded and it was simply an old building. Devoid of any emotion or impression, the Arena was nothing but stone and gravel, earth and sand.

Taking in the scene once again, Kaladin looked for the source of the musical tone that encompassed him. At the far end of the Arena, near one of the entrance archways, Kaladin saw a strange glowing light that was growing brighter, as if someone was carrying a torch through the tunnel out into the Arena. The light seemed to be the source of the music and it grew louder as it moved toward him.

Spilling out into the Arena, the light accompanied a lone figure emerging from the archway. The light didn't come from a torch, though. It was radiating from the body of the man walking toward Kaladin. Like a shimmering halo, the light seemed to permeate the entire Arena and Kaladin as well. Wherever the man stepped, the light seeped into the ground and brightened its appearance, making it look more detailed and colorful.

Kaladin could feel the entire atmosphere of the Arena change as the man approached him. The sky became a vivid shade of blue, the stone walls and columns looked bright and new, even the straw mats on the fighting platform felt softer under Kaladin's bare feet. Far from its heavy and dark ambience, the Arena had taken on a warm and inviting feeling. Kaladin knew that somehow, this person was able to change the environment however he pleased. The thought was both awesome and disquieting.

The figure stopped directly in front of Kaladin. Once his eyes had become accustomed to the glow, Kaladin could almost make out the man's features. He didn't recognize the face, but there was something very familiar about this person. Who are you? *Kaladin thought to himself.*

"*Someone who knows you well,*" *the figure replied quietly.*

Surprised his thoughts could be heard, Kaladin took a step back. "*But how…?*" *Kaladin whispered.*

"*You asked the question, this dream is the answer,*" *the man said.*

Kaladin was confused. "*What question?*"

"*You wanted to know where your anger came from, where your life was leading.*"

Kaladin was taken aback. "*And watching myself kill Valec, that's the answer?*"

"*What that experience tells you about yourself is the answer, Kaladin.*"

"*I don't understand. What is it supposed to tell me?*"

"*Only you know the answer. You'll have to figure it out for yourself.*"

Kaladin let the thought sink in. "*And where my life is leading me, what about that?*"

"*You are being shown choices, different paths that are open to you. The decisions you make will determine how your life unfolds. Your choices direct the difference between what could be and what will be.*"

The dream world was beginning to grow fuzzy and out of focus. "*But what do you mean? What are the choices?*" *Kaladin asked.*

The figure's features had dissolved into a shimmering outline of white light. "*Know who you are. All of who you are. Choose with awareness. In time you will understand.*" *The light swirled around Kaladin, enveloping him in its warm glow.*

❧

The strange music was still in his ears when Kaladin awoke under the crescent moon high above. Struggling to remember, Kaladin mumbled to himself. "Choices? What did he mean about choices? Know all of who I am..." He took a deep breath and pulled the blanket tighter around himself. Another moment passed, and he was asleep again.

CHAPTER 7

The next afternoon found Kaladin resuming his training with renewed enthusiasm. His dream, though only remembered in bits and pieces, had served to refuel his exploration of combat and his inner world.

He had stopped in a small moss-covered clearing near the water's edge to practice. The breeze flowing through the trees swirled past almost unnoticed as Kaladin twisted and turned in slow, deliberate movements. He circled about as if dancing or whirling in a trance. These were not the sharp, striking movements he had practiced in the past. They were a smooth, flowing expression of his body in space. Every motion had a distinct purpose, yet they all melted together so seamlessly that one movement appeared to *grow* from the next. It was an expression of *total harmony*. He was completely focused, totally intent on every movement he was making. In each moment, he was totally present, but it was as if his personality were an afterthought. The movements were expressing themselves through him. Kaladin was merely a channel for the energy.

Time seemed to stretch and distend as his training intensified. It almost felt as if traces of eternity were trickling into the world as he moved. He couldn't remember ever having felt so alive, so in touch with himself and nature.

Although he was focusing his attention on his movements, he could *feel* the environment around him almost as if it were his own body. He was the swaying reed, moving to and fro in the light breeze. He was the strong trunk of the tree nearby, solid, grounded and centered. He was the rolling current of the river, as it effortlessly made its way downstream. Each aspect of Kaladin's surroundings came alive through his training; it all felt like a part of him.

Suddenly Kaladin's concentration was broken by the sound of hoof beats. He looked downstream to see two men riding toward him on huge black horses that lumbered through the shallow water along the riverbank, spraying water with every stride. The riders, large men wrapped in animal skins, were a fearsome pair.

The taller of the two men rode up toward Kaladin while the other wheeled to the side, stopping along the water's edge.

"What are you doing out here, little man?" the tall horseman demanded.

"I'm just passing through," Kaladin calmly replied, feeling the waves of tranquility beginning to diminish. "I was just stopping to do some training. I'll be on my way soon."

"What sort of training?" the big man asked, resting his hand on the hilt of a large sword sheathed at his side.

Kaladin hesitated. He had been reluctant to speak of his abilities since his failure with the Council and was unsure what to say.

"Well?" the horseman prodded.

"Combat training," Kaladin answered softly.

The man laughed. "Combat? You? Show me some of your skills."

Kaladin drew a slow breath. "Perhaps another day."

"You'll show me now, whether you want to or not." He dismounted and stopped in front of Kaladin. Like heat from a fire, Kaladin could feel the hostility radiating from him.

"Please, I don't want any trouble," Kaladin implored him.

"That will all depend on how well you can fight." The man scowled down at Kaladin, who was a full head shorter.

Kaladin realized that negotiation was useless and that a fight was inevitable. He took a step back, lowered his hands to his sides and locked his eyes on his opponent.

The horseman balled up his fists and lunged at Kaladin, swinging first with his left, then his right. Kaladin pivoted smoothly past each punch and circled behind his opponent. The man spun around to find Kaladin waiting for his next move.

This time he kicked at Kaladin, who once again slipped to the side, avoiding the blow. Kaladin sidestepped another kick, then scooped his arm under his opponent's leg and shoved the big fellow off balance.

The man hit the ground with a mighty thud and lay still, momentarily dazed. Kaladin looked around the clearing briefly to see the other horseman staring in shocked disbelief from the riverbank.

The tall man rose to his feet, growled angrily at Kaladin and launched another attack. Once again, Kaladin sent him tumbling onto the ground, scattering leaves and clods of dirt.

Enraged, the man drew his sword and began to swing it at Kaladin, who easily evaded each blow. Soon the swordsman lost his balance and fell once again, face down in the earth. Kaladin stepped back as the large man mustered the strength to return to his feet once more. With a wild swing, he lunged at Kaladin's head. Kaladin caught the brute's sword hand and it twisted around, causing the weapon to drop to the ground. Kaladin pressed down, folding his opponent's arm against his body, doubling the man over. The horseman struggled to free himself in vain. His shoulder joint was locked into an extremely painful position. He was helpless and he knew it.

Because Kaladin had no intention of hurting his opponent, he released the pressure slightly.

Seeing all this, the other rider galloped to the aid of his companion. Kaladin saw him coming and in a split second, spun both himself and his captive around in a tight circle. He then hurled his captive toward the other horseman.

The impact caught the second rider totally by surprise. He was instantly knocked off his horse, end over end, into the chilly water. The first horseman flew well past his companion, striking the river's surface chest-first, throwing a huge spray of water into the air.

Kaladin surveyed the situation and saw that the men were no longer a threat to him. They shivered in the cold water, their faces red with the shame of having lost the fight...and perhaps their horses as well. Nothing remained of the two mounts but a rapidly fading cloud of dust in the distance.

Gathering his belongings, Kaladin took one last look and headed downstream. The two horsemen would have bigger things to worry about than him, and he was glad that the entire confrontation had resulted in nothing more destructive than a bump on the head and a couple of soaked egos. His abilities were indeed changing.

As he began to hike his way deeper into the forest, Kaladin wondered to himself; *Am I doing this, or is something doing it through me?* He recognized that whatever was happening to him, even if he didn't fully understand it, was something to be grateful for. Making his way through the trees and into the early evening twilight, Kaladin could only wonder what new skills were yet waiting to be discovered.

CHAPTER 8

A cool breeze woke Kaladin from his sleep under a large pine tree. Winter would be coming soon, and the chilly air reminded him that he would have to begin looking for some shelter. Following the river's path for the last several weeks had failed to bring Kaladin any closer to civilization. Today he decided to head away from the river in hopes of finding a settlement before the colder weather came to stay.

Yawning, Kaladin rolled over and rubbed his eyes.

"Good morning, Kaladin," a voice said. "Did you sleep well?"

Kaladin jumped back with a start as he realized that he was not alone. Twenty feet away, a man dressed in dark yellow robes sat quietly, observing him.

His heart racing, Kaladin squinted and looked more closely. The man had wavy gray hair, a modest beard and green eyes. He was sitting cross-legged against a large tree and an air of peaceful contentment seemed to radiate from his body. He didn't appear to be a threat, but Kaladin didn't want any surprises.

"*Who* are you…and how do you know my name?" Kaladin asked as he cautiously studied the stranger.

"My name is Tyban," the man said calmly. "As for how I know yours, well, that's a little difficult to explain right now. Nevertheless, I'm very glad I've found you."

"Found me? You've been *looking* for me?" Kaladin's mind began to spin. Had he been followed from the Thelius? Perhaps he had been tracked down so he could be captured or killed. Kaladin looked around, fully awake now; ready to run or fight if he had to.

Tyban sensed Kaladin's tension. "Please relax. I'm not here to hurt you. I've come to help you; to ask you to join us, if you choose."

"Join you? Join who? Join what? *Where did you come from?*" While Kaladin's fear had eased slightly, he was becoming deeply confused about just what was going on.

"Let me explain," Tyban said. "We've been watching you for quite some time now, since before you were cast out of the city many months ago."

Kaladin stared in dumbfounded silence, not knowing what to say or think.

"Like you, I come from a race of warriors. We too used to fight as you did, hurting, killing, being enslaved by our emotions; trapped by restrictive rules and old beliefs. But we found another way, Kaladin: a means of combat that liberates us from our old beliefs. We've learned to transcend the boundaries that held us prisoner for so long, and in doing so we've become free. You too, have begun down this path of enlightened combat, and that is why I am here."

Kaladin drew in a long breath. While what he was hearing made sense, it was a little hard to swallow all at once, first thing in the morning. "You mean there are more people who train and fight the way I do?" he asked.

"Yes. That's what brought you here, isn't it, the need to join with those of a like mind and spirit?"

Kaladin let the words sink in. Gradually, over the period of a few moments he slowly came to the realization that what he was hearing meant he wasn't alone. There were others who thought as he did! Others who might be able to teach him what he needed to learn and help him understand where his path was leading.

The fear and confusion Kaladin had felt a few minutes before dissolved into an insatiable curiosity. "Tell me more," Kaladin implored.

"What if I *show* you instead?" Tyban replied.

"Yes, please!"

"Then gather your things and come with me."

Kaladin paused momentarily, remembering the necessity of finding shelter.

"Come with you where?" was Kaladin's reply. He felt a pang of uncertainty in his stomach. Despite Tyban's apparent knowledge and tempting offer, Kaladin didn't know this person. After his encounter with the horsemen, it would be wise to be wary of strangers.

"You needn't be afraid, Kaladin. I have come to help you, that is, *if* you want it," Tyban said.

"How do I know I can trust you?" Kaladin asked.

"What do your instincts tell you?" Tyban asked, stroking his beard.

Kaladin paused. There was something vaguely familiar about this man, a mysterious quality that seemed just out of reach.

"I feel I should go with you, but I can't say why."

"Then why not walk with me? There will be time for you to find shelter later."

Kaladin's eyes widened. "How did you know I was looking for shelter?"

"Just a guess," Tyban replied.

Kaladin somehow thought otherwise, but for the time being he was convinced. "Alright," he said slowly. He collected his few belongings, and stomped out the embers of the fire.

"I'm ready."

The two walked into the forest and followed a narrow path up a gradually increasing slope. The trees were thick and the sun shone through their branches in gold spears that pierced the green and brown of the woodland floor.

"Let me ask you a question, Kaladin," Tyban said as he led the way through the hilly terrain.

"I thought I would be the one asking questions," Kaladin replied.

Tyban laughed. "There will be time for that later. But now, answer me this: What is it you are looking for?"

Kaladin was puzzled. "Looking for? I'm not sure I understand what you mean."

Tyban went on, "Do you believe that everything you've been through, your training, meditation, the fight and exile, were simply a cruel twist of fate or might there be another reason behind it all?"

Hearing Tyban describe the events of Kaladin's past with such clarity was slightly unnerving and it caught him off guard. After a pause he said, "Well, no. I guess I'm responsible for what brought me here. I made those choices."

"But why, what is it that you are seeking? Why did you make *those* choices? You must be searching for something…"

Kaladin paused again and reflected for a moment.

"A new form of combat?" Tyban asked.

"No…more than that. I know there is something greater to be discovered, I'm just not sure what it is. I guess it's not *just* a different way of fighting, but more like a different way of being."

Smiling softly, Tyban seemed satisfied with Kaladin's answer. "There *is* something greater indeed, Kaladin. And you have been moving in the right direction. Soon we will see if you are ready to take the next step."

They continued hiking through the forest as the slope grew steeper and jagged edges of stone began to peek through the moss-covered ground.

"You see, Kaladin, you are just beginning to wake up to the journey we are all on," Tyban continued. "Every warrior is climbing the ladder of enlightened combat. Some choose to climb slowly, to stay at a particular level and enjoy the view at that height for as long as they please. Others, like yourself, keep pushing ahead, learning more and more, never satisfied until they find all the answers to all their questions."

Kaladin smiled to himself. He could feel the truth of which Tyban spoke. He secretly hoped that he would never stop learning and he couldn't imagine an end of his explorations. "But how high does the ladder go?" Kaladin asked.

"However high you want it to go. There are realms of reality that reach out farther than you are able to imagine."

"Realms of reality?" Kaladin reached forward to steady himself as he stepped over a rotting tree trunk.

"With time you will begin to understand, Kaladin." Tyban gestured to their surroundings. "This solid and seemingly fixed reality is only one of many different ways of experiencing the world."

"And you say I'm just at the beginning? But it feels as if I've come so far," Kaladin insisted.

"We shall see," Tyban replied. "Knowing the distance you travel depends on having a point of comparison. But eventually, comparison won't be necessary."

Kaladin's mind had begun to boggle a bit. "So there's no limit to what I can make my body do?"

"That depends on how you look at it," Tyban cautioned him. "All along, you've believed that the mind trains the body. But in reality, the mind *uses* the body to condition itself to believe what is possible. In focusing only upon *what is* or *what has been*, the mind traps itself into a prison of limited possibilities.

"The limits of your body are not written in the muscles and bones of your physical form. They exist *solely* in your mind. When you choose to focus on what you desire to the exclusion of all other thoughts, you let go of the limits you have placed upon reality, and a new world opens up to you."

Kaladin was growing confused. "A new world?"

"Indeed, Kaladin. The boundaries of time and space, the laws of nature; these too can be transcended, when you are ready."

"How soon is that?"

Tyban nodded and smiled. "That will depend upon you," he replied. "But rest assured, you're moving in the right direction."

"How did *you* learn these things?" Kaladin asked. The sun had disappeared behind a large cloud, causing the forest to grow noticeably cooler.

"Not unlike you have, Kaladin. We all have experiences that sooner or later push us forward into a new way of seeing the world. For me, that push came when I gave up the life of an army soldier. I was forced to serve under a tyrannical general, bent on destruction and needless violence. One fateful day, after a brutal skirmish that left hundreds dead on the battlefield, I deserted the army and vowed to be more than a murderer's mindless puppet. In my solitude, I began to look for another way of combat *and* experiencing the world. That search led me to my teacher, a teacher who helped show me the path that would help me find the knowledge I sought."

"A *path?*" Kaladin's curiosity beamed in his eyes.

"Yes. By choosing to become *conscious* of their own level of growth and development, a warrior's journey, although not necessarily easier, becomes more reliable; the outcome more predictable. Their journey is the path of the Enlightened Warrior."

"Can I follow this path? Will you teach me?" Kaladin pressed Tyban.

"We shall see," Tyban repeated once again. "If you are ready, perhaps."

"I am; I *must* be!" Kaladin pleaded.

"Hmmm, so eager you are. When I found you, all that mattered was finding shelter. Now you're ready to devote your life to a path of enlightened combat? Know yourself, Kaladin; know yourself well, for in that knowing shall you understand what your heart truly desires."

Kaladin continued to climb in silence as he considered what Tyban had said. Inexplicably, this stranger seemed to be able to see deep into Kaladin's being. It was a somewhat uncomfortable feeling, but despite the oddness of it all, Kaladin knew that there was more to Tyban than met the eye. Time would tell.

CHAPTER 9

Kaladin had been silent for a long while, and eventually he and Tyban stopped in a clearing along the edge of a large grass-covered slope. "You don't strike me as a warrior," Kaladin said at last. "You have this serenity about you that I've never experienced before. No offense, but all the warriors I've ever known have seemed much tougher."

"I would imagine so." Tyban smiled.

"Aren't warriors supposed to be strong and powerful?"

"Are they?" Tyban looked quizzically at Kaladin. "I guess someone forgot to tell me."

The lightness of Tyban's tone indicated that he was both half-joking and half-serious at the same time.

"At a particular level of development, Kaladin, appearances can be very important and convincing. People rely on them as *The Truth*, when in fact they are simply only an aspect of a much deeper truth. It's like mistaking a map for the territory. A drawing can never do justice to the beauty of a landscape, the depth of an ocean. People are no different. The mask of a physical body easily hides what lies beneath the surface. From where I sit, a warrior who appears non-threatening and at peace is much more evolved than one who glares in intimidation and anger. Far more important than the outward appearance is the *intention* behind it."

Kaladin thought hard about that. "I'll have to let that one sink in for a while," he said.

"You do that."

Kaladin looked down into the valley, over the forest they had climbed through. It was warmer on the grassy plateau, away from the trees, and the sound of the river was nothing but a distant murmur. Turning to look further uphill, he heard a rustling in the bushes nearby that made him look closer.

Slowly and cautiously from beneath a tree limb approached a large brown mountain lion. It took several careful steps out off the bushes and looked around attentively. Peering to its left, its narrow green eyes focused intently upon Kaladin and Tyban.

Kaladin froze in his tracks. He suddenly remembered stories of lions like this attacking along the outer frontier of Arkana when he was a child. Entire villages had been wiped out and many brave warriors bore the scars of fighting off the powerful beasts.

With his heart pounding in his chest, Kaladin dared not move. Glancing out of the corner of his eye toward Tyban, he hoped his companion would know what to do. To Kaladin's surprise, though, Tyban was simply smiling calmly at the huge cat.

The mountain lion waited, its large paws pressing down into the dried leaves, tail swishing against the tall grass.

Suddenly, and to Kaladin's great surprise, the giant cat let out a low sigh. Half-growl, half-moan, the sound wasn't something one would expect from a man-eating lion. The cat looked from side to side, sniffed the air, and strolled toward Kaladin and Tyban.

Gasping, Kaladin took a step back, but in his haste, he stumbled and fell backward onto the ground. By now the lion had nearly reached them. Kaladin looked to Tyban for help, but Tyban was just standing there, his smile growing.

The lion strode right up to Tyban and to Kaladin's shock, rubbed against his leg and nuzzled his hand with its head.

Mountain lions don't act this way, Kaladin thought to himself in alarm. At that, the lion turned to Kaladin, lying frozen on the ground like a statue, and rubbed its head against his. With his eyes as wide as saucers, Kaladin sat helplessly as the huge cat brushed its whiskers over his face.

After a few moments the lion seemed satisfied with Kaladin and turned to saunter gently off into the grass behind them. Kaladin watched in amazement as the beast pawed past him, its tail thumping him in the chest as it went.

Extending his hand to his prone companion, Tyban helped Kaladin to his feet.

"How…how did that happen?" Kaladin stammered out, trying to calm his pounding heart.

"Wasn't what it appeared to be, was it," Tyban asked.

"No…it wasn't," Kaladin was still stunned.

"Now you see that what's on the surface can betray the reality lying beneath."

"Yes, I guess so," Kaladin replied tentatively. "But that's not how mountain lions are supposed to behave."

"According to who?" Tyban questioned. "You? Your experiences? The experiences of others?"

Kaladin had no answer as his mind stumbled around for something to hold onto.

Tyban continued, "Who can say why a mountain lion doesn't attack in the middle of his natural environment? Perhaps he just had a big meal, maybe he was tired, or he possibly didn't find us appetizing. Regardless of the reason, the lion didn't attack us because he had no desire to do so. Your fear was based upon his appearance, not upon his intentions, and you reacted to that fear. Learn to see beyond appearances, for they can trap you in the known. Be willing to experience the unknown and you will begin to see the world through different eyes."

Kaladin stared in amazement at his companion as Tyban turned to continue the climb along the hillside. *This is going to be an interesting journey*, Kaladin thought as he turned to follow.

"Can you show me how *you* fight, Tyban?" Kaladin blurted out. An hour had passed and Kaladin was still entranced by the miracle of not being torn to shreds by the mountain lion and he had been aching to see what his companion was capable of. Deep down he wondered just how good Tyban was.

"I'm afraid not," Tyban said.

"But why? I want to learn more. How can I learn if you don't teach me what I need to do?"

"I never said I would teach you, Kaladin. Don't assume too much. I am simply here to open your mind to new possibilities. What you learn will be up to you. Do you understand?"

Kaladin felt like a child reprimanded by a stern parent. He nodded in agreement.

"Now, understand that I can't show you how I fight; because there is no one *here* to fight, no *reason* to fight. You are not my enemy or opponent and I have no desire to harm you or be harmed *by you*. Listen closely, Kaladin. Combat produces only destruction. Physical conflict is always the last option of the enlightened warrior. This is not merely a matter of flowery words. This is one of the high truths that we have come to understand."

"Oh, well, I didn't mean *real* fighting. I guess I meant combat practice."

"Yes, I know that." Tyban was smiling. "I just wanted to make that distinction right from the beginning. Remember that training in the fighting arts has only two goals: self-protection and self-perfection. And once you have perfected yourself, protecting yourself won't be necessary."

"I'm confused now," Kaladin said, shaking his head.

Tyban sat on an aged tree stump. "A long time ago, there lived a man who had once been a mighty warrior. A master swordsman, he had given up fighting to live alone as a peaceful farmer. He made his home on the outskirts of a small village and was content with his simple life.

"One day, though, word came from a neighboring village that a pack of barbarians was plundering the towns and killing settlers throughout the territory. Simple people, these villagers were far from the armies and protection of the big cities and had no means of defense against attackers. In their fear, they turned to the great swordsman for help.

"Please help us, protect us from the barbarians," they cried. The noble warrior listened with compassion and agreed to help, for having lived with them many years he loved the villagers as his family.

"Long since hidden, the master's sword was unsheathed so that he might practice again the ways of the warrior. Day and night he practiced, honing his skills, becoming at one with his art, his practice; preparing for the day when his abilities would be tested once more.

"Finally, one morning, the village bell rang out, warning all of the impending attack. The master, dressed in his simple farmer's clothing, walked to the edge of the village and waited while the frightened villagers looked on. To their surprise and horror, the master wasn't carrying his sword; he was completely unarmed, and totally defenseless.

"With a thunder of hoof beats and a cloud of dust, the barbarians descended upon the village but came to a sudden halt when they saw the master standing in their path.

"The master stood still and silent, softly gazing at the pack of killers and thieves. The barbarians looked at one another in confusion while the great warrior waited. The silence lasted for what seemed like an eternity as the barbarians stared at their adversary.

"In that endless moment, the leader of the barbarian horde saw something in the great warrior's eyes that was beyond words; beyond age or experience. Those eyes, still as a crystal lake, reflected like a mirror the barbarian's true self. In that instant, he saw himself clearly for the first time and was ashamed of what he was, and fearful of what he would become.

"Then suddenly, and without warning, the barbarian leader signaled for his men to withdraw from the village. They galloped away and left the master and his village in peace."

There was a long silence. Tyban asked "Do you understand now?"

Kaladin paused for a long time, thinking. "Perhaps I should ask you to show me how *not* to fight."

"Now, that I can do." Tyban smiled and adjusted his robes. "Let's begin with speed. Your goal will be quite simple. All I want you to do is touch me. However you choose, wherever you choose. Just a simple touch."

That sounded easy enough to Kaladin, knowing his speed was now far above average. He adjusted his position slightly in preparation, fixed his eyes on Tyban, standing a mere three feet away, and leaped forward.

Kaladin's hand flailed the empty air. He should have easily tapped Tyban's shoulder, but Tyban had somehow shifted around Kaladin and was standing nearly behind him. Kaladin spun around to face Tyban's smile.

"Try again," Tyban said.

Kaladin shot forward again, only to miss again. This time Tyban spun around Kaladin, until he stood exactly where he had began.

"Damn!" Kaladin mumbled to himself.

"Remember what I told you about limitations, Kaladin. They don't exist in time and space. They exist…." Kaladin lunged forward, hoping to catch Tyban unprepared in a burst of raw power and speed. His palm should have slammed into Tyban's chest, but Tyban wasn't there. Kaladin stumbled and tried to catch his balance. "…In your mind." Tyban's words echoed through the air.

Kaladin looked around for his companion, but he wasn't there. He spun around in a circle, expecting Tyban to be just outside of his view, but could find nothing.

"Looking for something?"

Kaladin reeled around to see Tyban sitting on a rocky outcropping some 10 feet overhead. Kaladin's mouth fell open in stunned silence.

"Whoa…"

"All in your mind, Kaladin. Moving from here to there doesn't need to be a matter of struggle or effort. It can be as simple as *thinking* from here…to here."

Kaladin looked over his shoulder to see Tyban standing right next to him. "It's difficult to be hit when you're not there, isn't it?" Tyban sat down on the grass.

"This isn't possible," Kaladin whispered.

"Once you change the level of your perception, *anything* is possible, Kaladin."

"And how do I do that?"

"Practice…and patience," Tyban replied.

"But, but what do I practice?" Kaladin couldn't imagine how one could acquire such amazing abilities.

"Thinking faster." Tyban paused for a moment. "See yourself moving at unlimited speed in your mind's eye, and over time, your body will act accordingly. Are you hungry?"

The subject change caught Kaladin by surprise. "Hungry? Well...I suppose, but I really want to learn more of this non-fighting of yours."

"There will be plenty of time for that," Tyban assured Kaladin. "Let's eat." He reached into the folds of his robes and produced a leather sack containing rice cakes, nuts and dried fruit. "Help yourself."

Kaladin thanked Tyban and savored the food. His diet over the last few months had been sparse and he was grateful to enjoy a nourishing meal with his new companion.

After eating, the two resumed their climb, taking a path that led up a tall mountain. Kaladin had no idea where they were headed, but he was feeling more confident that he could trust Tyban. In spite of the short time they had been together, Kaladin was beginning to feel as if he and Tyban were old friends. It puzzled him, but while he couldn't explain it, the strange familiarity put him at ease. The months alone had left him desperately wanting for like-minded others. Now it seemed he had found, or had been found by, such a like-minded person who clearly held the key to the knowledge Kaladin sought.

CHAPTER 10

The late afternoon sun, nearing the horizon, was peeking from behind a few scattered clouds. Kaladin and Tyban were following a narrow path that gently spiraled upward around a large rock face. Quietly thinking to himself for the last hour, Kaladin had been considering his interesting companion and wondered where he would lead them.

"Tell me more about conquering limitations, Tyban."

"We don't 'conquer' our limitations in a fighting sense, Kaladin. We simply climb to a level of development where certain limitations no longer apply."

A chilly breeze rustled through the large fir trees that dotted the mountain path.

"So what I see as a boundary or limit is related to my level of growth?"

"Exactly. At one time your level of development made it appear that the boundaries of style and tradition were fixed and immovable. But as you grew, you came to understand that they were merely outdated ways of thinking that were no longer appropriate to whom you had become. In doing so, they lost their power over you. Likewise, other so-called laws and boundaries will fall away as you rise above the beliefs that hold them in place."

"Do you mean that laws, limitations and boundaries only serve to restrict people," Kaladin asked.

Tyban paused along the path to turn to Kaladin. "Yes and no. Limitations and boundaries are necessary because they create the structure of the world and society people live in. Without them there would be total chaos. They create a framework from which to build on. However, when you use your limitations as stepping-stones for growth, they become the keys to set you free. For example when you began to study the martial arts, what was the first thing you were taught?"

"Stances, of course," Kaladin replied. He recalled his first days of training with his father in their small family practice hall and the importance that was placed on a strong and balanced base from which attacks could be delivered.

"Yes," Tyban said. "You had to learn the basic structure, the subtle boundaries of a solid body position before you could attempt any attack or defense. Without those basic and firm principles of a strong stance, you would have ended up flat on your face when throwing the simplest punch."

Kaladin nodded in understanding. "But once I understood those principles and laws of body positioning, I was free to perform more difficult movements."

"Yes!" Tyban grinned. Those initial limitations served to help you build a strong foundation, but once it was in place, you learned that some of those rules could be bent and even broken, right?"

"Yes, I see that," Kaladin said.

"The same applies to all boundaries and limitations everywhere. The important thing is that they unfold with your abilities in a progression. One thing at a time, step by step."

"How will I know what level I'm at?"

"Certain clues along the way will give you an idea of how far you've traveled along the path."

The trail turned left and began to wind along a steep ledge overlooking the lush valley below. The gray rock face sparkled with moisture that trickled down the hillside from far above.

"Clues?" Kaladin looked upward. The sky above them looked like a narrow unrolled blue ribbon. He felt very small.

"Well, for example, your intentions and desires. The things that are important to you will change as you grow. At the lowest level of development, a warrior is concerned only with the most basic and primal urges of survival and dominance over another. Staying alive is all that matters. Like a cunning animal, this warrior relies on his physical abilities simply to keep himself alive.

"As his strength and skill increase, though, he moves to the next level, which emphasizes control and competition. This level is all about proving oneself. A warrior doesn't fight to ensure the survival of the body, but rather the survival of the self-image."

Kaladin thought back to his days in the Arena. He remembered how the fights were about nothing other than survival and competition. What Tyban was saying made perfect sense.

The path turned sharply toward the left. As they made their way along the trail Kaladin could hear the sound of rushing water from a nearby mountain stream.

Tyban continued. "At the next level, things shift more toward understanding and a conscious sense of growth and progress. A warrior at this level looks within to seek out the truest expression of himself that he can be. Knowing that there is something beyond survival and competition, he takes the first steps toward mastering himself through his art."

"Now the warrior has begun to see the edges of his own self-imposed frontier. He knows that there is more to life than simply *The Fight* and in doing so has developed a respect for all life. He lets compassion rather than anger dominate an encounter. He desires harmony and peace to be a part of his everyday life. This level brings with it an inner calm and awareness that extends out into the larger world."

"I've felt that!" Kaladin exclaimed.

"Yes, Kaladin. And now the warrior chooses to make it a conscious experience, rather than a fleeting sensation. As you develop that feeling, it will grow to become your natural state."

"What comes next?" Kaladin implored, hungry for more.

Tyban smiled at Kaladin's enthusiasm. "Next is the creation of something totally new, totally unique to the individual. Inspiration drives the warrior to attain a way of being never known before. That expression becomes the warrior's own 'art.' He wants nothing more than to bring his creation into expression."

"And then?"

"At the next stage, the warrior uses his personal art as a vehicle to carry him past the boundaries of this world. He is able to see beyond the reality that we have all grown to accept as unchanging. This is where the warrior's skills go far beyond what we are able to imagine. Transcending the rules of reality itself, a warrior at this stage becomes superhuman.

"Finally, in the last level of development, the warrior knows no boundaries or limits and simply desires to be. He has become one with the mind of the universe and is a total expression of the enlightened warrior."

Kaladin looked puzzled. "So in the end, the warrior *just is*? That sounds rather dull."

"Only from your perspective, Kaladin. In the eyes of an enlightened warrior, the world is his canvas and he can paint it however he sees fit. He has total mastery over his body, mind and spirit. Far from dull, it is the most exciting and advanced experience of being alive."

"But what does one do at that level? Is he still a warrior or something…different?" Kaladin asked.

"A warrior, yes, but of a different kind."

"What do you mean?" Kaladin felt lost along the wall of towering granite. The sound of the rushing stream was growing louder.

"At this stage, physical confrontations dissolve in the boundlessness of pure love, pure light."

"Love?" Kaladin said. "I've never thought that love was a quality of a warrior."

"Haven't you?" Tyban questioned. "Do you not love your art?"

"Well, yes, but that's different."

"No, it's not. Instead of perceiving your love as limited to one particular object, imagine that love shining over everything and everyone in the entire universe."

Kaladin sighed deeply and shook his head.

"What's the matter?" Tyban asked.

"It's just so much. I think I'm having a hard time grasping it all."

"I see," Tyban replied. "Perhaps I can make it a little easier for you to understand."

Ahead, the mountain wall curved into itself, forming a narrow recess. The sound of rushing water filled Kaladin's ears as he beheld a beautiful waterfall cascading from far overhead. The waterfall had gradually dug its way into the mountainside over hundreds of years. Winding its way behind the falls, the path led Tyban and Kaladin beneath the large rock overhang from where the icy mountain stream poured on its journey to the river far below.

The sunlight shimmered through the clear liquid curtain, creating a cool glow throughout the recess. Tyban sat down cross-legged on a granite slab in front of a large pool of water and motioned for Kaladin to do the same. Kaladin took his seat next to his companion, enjoying the opportunity to rest for a moment. Tyban, staring into the water, seemed to be lost in thought.

"The levels of a warrior's development," Tyban broke the silence, "are all aspects of one unifying whole. Like water," he swished his hand through the pool near his feet, "those levels take on different forms to fulfill a certain purpose."

Kaladin listened intently to his companion as the rush of the waterfall faded into the background.

"Water can take on many differing shapes and each one of those forms is like a particular level of a warrior's development. For example, pouring, crashing water, such as in this waterfall, can be destructive. It smashes through all obstacles with no regard for the damage or harm it may cause. This is like the warrior in the earliest level of development. He is brutal and deadly, with no concern for anything other than his own survival.

"Water can also be predictable," Tyban went on. He reached down and swished his hand through the water, creating a ripple that reached the far side of the pool and rolled back to Kaladin's feet, washing over the edge and onto the rock slab. Kaladin pulled his feet back so as not to get wet.

"This is just like a warrior of the second level, who acts in a predictable, conditioned manner, striving to protect his own ego. He reacts just like the water; when pushed, he pushes back in response."

Kaladin was beginning to see a pattern forming.

"Look over there, to the far edge of the pool."

Near the rocky lip of the pool a small current of water flowed over the edge of the ledge and into the gorge below.

Next to the channel was a small whirlpool, calmly spiraling downward.

Tyban drew little circles in the air. "You see how the whirlpool goes within, spinning around and inward, undisturbed by the flowing water right next to it?"

Kaladin nodded in agreement.

"Similarly, the warrior in the third stage goes within to know his own nature, rather than relying on an outside authority, the past or his conditioning."

Fascinated by Tyban's analogy, Kaladin continued to listen with rapt attention.

"Now imagine a flowing river, quietly, calmly flowing toward the sea. Harmonious, flowing and peaceful, seeking the path of least resistance, it nourishes and protects life as it goes."

"This is like the warrior in the fourth stage. He wishes to harm no one. Instead, he is supportive and flowing, peaceful and intuitive."

The late afternoon sun was casting an orange glow through the cascading water and onto the rock walls surrounding Kaladin and Tyban. Nightfall wouldn't be far off, but Kaladin didn't care. He was captivated by Tyban's explanation.

"What happens when you put water in a cup?" Tyban asked.

Kaladin thought for a moment. "It fills the cup."

"Yes, and?"

Kaladin cocked his head in understanding. "It takes on the shape of the cup."

"Exactly," Tyban replied. "Not only that, but it takes on the shape of whatever container it finds itself in. It is able to shape itself however it sees fit. The warrior at the next level has the same ability. He molds and creates himself into something new and unique."

"Amazing." Kaladin whispered. "I'm beginning to understand."

"Good, then tell me what comes next. What other form can water take?"

Kaladin looked around. The water rushing down into the gorge splashed on the rocks as it fell, kicking up a cloud of mist that swirled through the air. A light breeze blew softly through the gorge and the spray lightly tickled his face.

"The mist!" Kaladin exclaimed. "The mist can blow and swirl through the air. It can even fly."

"Indeed," Tyban replied. "There are few limits to where it can go and what it may do. And like mist, the warrior at the sixth level is capable of new and amazing abilities. Things you would consider impossible and miraculous become commonplace."

"Lastly," Tyban concluded, "water is truly everywhere. It's in the air we breathe, in the plants, in the clouds. It is a *part* of everything and *sustains* everything. Likewise, the warrior at this last level is one with all. Nurturing and flowing through everything, he quietly guides and supports all beings on their path to higher understanding."

"It's incredible," Kaladin said as he traced his fingers through the chilly water.

"It will be even more incredible when you actually experience it, trust me," Tyban replied. "Come on, just a little further now." He rose and followed the path out from behind the waterfall and back out onto the opposite ledge. Kaladin sipped some water and followed, emerging from the falls to see the valley below shaded in the shadows of the setting sun. The rolling hills beneath them were stretched out in a red and orange patchwork, displaying the autumn colors.

The pair continued along the path as it extended along the mountainside. Ahead, a neighboring mountain pressed hard against the edge of the path, forcing the narrow trail into a tight crevasse between the two granite walls.

Tyban paused for a moment, seemingly to survey the situation. He smiled lightly and turned into the opening. Kaladin followed closely, the last rays of sunlight fading behind the tree-covered hilltops.

The passage twisted and turned, becoming narrower as it curved deeply between the two mountains. The fading daylight, trickling through the top of the fissure, was barely enough to light the way for Kaladin, but Tyban continued forward without difficulty. At long last, the crevasse came to a dead end in a large, cave-like chamber. Open to the night sky above, the chamber was lit with a soft blue glow from the rising full moon.

Kaladin looked around. Seeing no way out, he threw a puzzled look at Tyban and wondered what would come next.

Tyban looked over to Kaladin and winked. "So, are you ready?"

"For what?" Kaladin stared in anticipation.

"To take your first step into a larger world?"

Kaladin looked around. "Here?"

"Kaladin," Tyban turned to him, "the world is far more than you imagine it to be. "This," he gestured toward their surroundings, "is only one aspect of a much larger whole."

He silently stretched out his hand until it rested on the rock wall. Instead of touching solid rock, though, Tyban's hand pushed up against the rock surface, sending ripples through the stone like pebbles thrown into a pond.

Kaladin's eyes widened in amazement as his new friend drew circles in the rock-water in front of them. "Still ready?" Tyban asked.

"Uh...yes." Kaladin's brow tightened a bit. Despite being amazed by what he saw, a trickle a fear ran though his body, making his breath catch in his throat.

"Then follow me." With that, Tyban took a step forward and pushed his hand, then arm, then shoulder into the liquid rock. Then, without warning, he leaned forward and disappeared into the wall, leaving Kaladin alone.

Gasping, Kaladin stared at the spot where Tyban had been and then at the wall. It was still rippling following Tyban's passage.

Limitations are all in my mind... Kaladin repeated mantra-like to himself as he stepped closer to the rock. He touched the wall and it shook just as before. He paused for a moment, astonished to watch his hand creating waves in a wall of stone. He laughed out loud. *This can't be happening, I can't believe it,* he said to himself.

Suddenly, the ripples rolling through the rock wall froze. Kaladin's hand pushed up against the wall, but it no longer was liquid. The ripples and waves were petrified in the wall, unmoving and solid.

Kaladin jumped back in surprise. He looked around the wall's edges, and then slapped his hand up against the stone, only to feel the cold solid rock under his fingers.

"What?" Kaladin muttered to himself. "What happened? Hello...Tyban?" Kaladin felt foolish. He was talking to a wall.

Panic and frustration clutched at Kaladin's chest as he pounded his fists against the rock. "No! No, no, no...wait..." His voice trickled off into silence as his forehead rested up against the cool granite.

Now what do I do? he wondered to himself. He spun around, leaning his back against the wall, and slid down to the ground. Overwhelmed by the thought of having traveled so far only to be left behind, Kaladin hung his head between his knees and sighed deeply. The sound of his breath echoed through the chamber as it filled his lungs.

Thinking back over the obstacles in his recent past made him feel even more helpless. *I give up*, he thought to himself as he closed his eyes.

As he sat alone in the cold chamber, an odd sensation began to run up his spine. Kaladin barely noticed it at first, but as it gained intensity, he became aware of a warm tingling sensation throughout his back. Turning his head, Kaladin realized the wall had become fluid once more and his shoulder blade was dipping into the liquid rock. Without the solidity of the wall to hold him up, he struggled to maintain his balance, but it was no use.

"Ahhh," Kaladin gasped and he tumbled backward into the dark unknown…

CHAPTER 11

Lying flat on his back, Kaladin reached up to rub his eyes. Formless blotches of color floated through his field of vision. As he looked around and struggled to get up, he could see nothing but a hazy outline of shapes and images. He squeezed his eyes tightly together and opened them again. This time the images had grown clearer. In another moment his vision had returned to normal. But where he found himself didn't seem normal at all. The mountain had disappeared completely and Kaladin found himself kneeling on the edge of a beach, stretching as far as he could see. To his right was a softly sloping hill covered with trees. To the left was nothing but sparkling water gently lapping at his feet. A thin layer of clouds covered the sky, reaching out to the horizon. Kaladin was very confused indeed.

"Well done, Kaladin. For a moment there I thought you weren't coming."

Kaladin was relieved to see Tyban crouching on a narrow footpath along the edge of the hill.

"How do you feel?" Tyban asked.

Still fighting off his disorientation, Kaladin managed to nod at his companion. "All right, I guess," he said groggily. "I didn't think I was going to make it," Kaladin said.

"You had me worried there for a minute," Tyban replied.

"What happened?" Kaladin asked. "Why couldn't I just walk through like you did?"

"Perhaps it had something to do with you doubting yourself."

"Doubting myself?"

"Yes," Tyban said. "Walking through a wall becomes impossible *the moment* you cease to believe that you can do it." You must learn to trust, to believe that anything can happen, that miracles do exist."

"Miracles," Kaladin whispered to himself.

"Miracles, Kaladin. Why do so few people experience them? Because they doubt their existence. If more people believed in them, perhaps they would experience the miraculous more often. Tell yourself you can't do something with enough conviction and you'll make it true. Are you sure you're alright?"

"Yeah." Kaladin rose to his feet and walked to the water's edge. He dipped his hand in a wave and splashed the water on his face. It was clean and cool. He was standing along the edge of an enormous fresh water lake.

"What an odd sensation that was, though." He turned to face Tyban. "Almost like I was everywhere all at once, if that makes sense."

Tyban smiled. "Yes, it does. And that's a pretty good guess. Don't worry, you get used to it after a while. As a matter of fact, you'll probably come to enjoy it."

For the first time, Kaladin took a long look around at his surroundings. "Tyban, what is this place? Where are we? The mountain...I thought..."

"That you were just going *into* the mountain? Or that you were going *through* it?"

"I don't know what I thought. But I know *it* wasn't *this*... whatever this is." Kaladin trudged through the sand toward his friend.

"This place, Kaladin, like any other, is a particular layer of reality out of the infinity that makes up the whole of everything in existence. All of these layers will be within your reach whenever you open yourself up to them. The mountain just happened to be a convenient place to open a door, a door that could lead to any number of worlds, not just here. Technically speaking, you don't even need a wall, but I didn't want you to be overwhelmed."

"Too late," Kaladin jabbed back. "My head is spinning."

Tyban laughed, "Come on, let me show you around."

They started up the path through a small grove of trees. Kaladin's mind had begun to clear considerably, and he had grown increasingly curious with every step. "So how far are we from where we started, Tyban?"

"That all depends on how you look at it. From one point of view, we haven't moved at all, from another we are as distant as the farthest star. Where we are isn't a matter of distance. It's a matter of…"

"Perception?" Kaladin responded.

"Exactly! Go on."

"Well, are you saying that by removing self-imposed boundaries, we can travel anywhere, anytime, at limitless speed?" Kaladin's tone betrayed a hint of sarcasm. It seemed too simple, too good to be true.

"Basically, yes."

"It sure sounds good anyway…" Kaladin replied.

"What?" Tyban stopped along the path to stare wide-eyed at Kaladin.

"Well, it sounds so simple, but if it were so easy, why isn't everyone walking through mountains?"

Tyban's tone became more serious. "Because, Kaladin, often the simplest truths require lifetimes of discipline to master. You have much to learn, not only about your art, but also about what you know of yourself and the world. Don't take for granted that it often takes much practice before what was once difficult becomes easy."

Kaladin was taken aback slightly by his friend's reproach. "But how do you *do* it?"

Tyban sighed, "Like anything else, Kaladin, with practice and patience. On your first day you're traveling to far-flung worlds and you still want more? The details will come in time, my friend. Try not to get ahead of yourself."

"Sorry." Kaladin could feel he was pushing Tyban for answers, but he so wanted to learn, to really feel what Tyban was telling him.

"You'll know things when you're *ready* to know them. There's a reason for everything. You learn at the pace you are best suited for. Going faster than that would simply overwhelm you, and perhaps even drive you insane, and you certainly wouldn't learn anything that way. Understanding the big picture is best achieved by looking at how the smaller pieces make up the whole over time. But remember, *time* is only as real as you make it."

His mind unable to process it all, Kaladin fell silent as they continued up the hill. The light was fading as large clouds covered the sky. For a moment Kaladin paused to wonder why the sun hadn't yet set in this place. But considering what he had just experienced along with the growing wave of exhaustion that washed over his body, he was willing to take a few things on faith.

They came out of the small cluster of trees into an open area, which was obviously a settlement. Small wooden cabins lined a central path running around the edge of a wide green valley. A large stone structure stood at the far end. With huge stone columns flanking the solid wooden doors and powerful stone walls sloping upward toward a domed roof, the building was obviously a temple, the focal point of the settlement.

Tyban and Kaladin had climbed a good distance up from the beach and a small grassy clearing near one of the cabins offered a beautiful view of the lake below. Lush vegetation and trees dotted throughout the settlement gave it a very welcoming appearance. Although Kaladin had never been there before, the place felt very familiar to him, almost as if he had dreamed it years ago.

The two made their way along the gravel pathway that circled the village. The settlement had a natural simplicity that struck Kaladin as very beautiful. At the same time, he could feel a silent power that seemed to flow through the very air itself.

"Is this where you're from?" Kaladin asked Tyban.

"It isn't where I was born, if that's what you mean, but it's what I call home now. It is called Lambec." Tyban smiled softly in a noticeable and genuine fondness for the place. He looked over at Kaladin, whose obvious curiosity couldn't conceal the tiredness he felt. "It's been a long day and you should get some rest. This way…"

Tyban led Kaladin up the pathway to the top edge of the valley, which overlooked the entire settlement. Torches flickered along the pathway, outlining the village in an orange glow.

They stopped at a small cabin that was tucked against a few large trees overlooking the beach below. Tyban opened the door and ushered Kaladin inside. A few candles lit the modest dwelling and threw shadows onto the bed in the corner.

"Get some sleep, tomorrow will be a big day," Tyban whispered.

"What do you mean?" Kaladin asked.

"Tomorrow you meet your fellow warriors."

"I do?" Kaladin felt a wave of exhilaration flow through him.

"Yes." Tyban's tone deepened. "And we'll see what kind of warrior you are." With that, Tyban stepped outside and closed the door behind him, leaving Kaladin alone.

Barely audible inside the cabin, the waves from the lakeside below rolled in and out as Kaladin wondered what Tyban had meant. He was too tired to care, though. With heavy eyes, Kaladin lied down on the bed and fell into a deep sleep.

CHAPTER 12

The deep tonal ringing of an ancient bell woke Kaladin the next morning. It resounded several times throughout the settlement, signaling the start of a new day. Stretching off the night, Kaladin felt full of life and expectancy for what the day would hold.

He looked around the cabin lit by the morning sun streaming through the windows. A towel and wash basin filled with water rested on a small round table near the wall opposite the bed. Near the door sat a tray of food, and a white training uniform, neatly folded. Kaladin splashed some water on his face, changed clothes and hastily ate his breakfast. He was anxious to find Tyban and learn more about Lambec and the others who lived there.

Stepping out of the cabin, Kaladin hardly noticed Tyban sitting in meditation against the pillar of the porch.

"Hello," Tyban said in greeting.

"Tyban! Good morning," Kaladin replied enthusiastically.

"Ready to get started?" Tyban asked.

"I think so," Kaladin answered, not knowing exactly what to expect.

"Then let's be on our way." Tyban rose to his feet and gestured toward the gravel pathway.

They walked throughout the settlement, now brightly lit by the morning sun. Kaladin noticed that, unlike the quiet night before, Lambec was full of activity. People were coming and going throughout the village. Some were training in outdoor pavilions; others listened to a lecture in an amphitheater, while still others sat studying texts in small gardens.

Through wide and amazed eyes, Kaladin took in all the sights and sounds of this interesting place. Leading the way, Tyban pointed out buildings and pieces of training equipment that were scattered along the path.

Passers-by would smile or wave as they walked along, magnifying the serene power that Kaladin had felt the night before. Deep within him, Kaladin somehow knew this was where he belonged. This was what he had been seeking; a place that apparently valued those ideals that he had come to cherish, a place that his heart could call home.

Up ahead, the pathway departed from the open valley and entered into a thick glade of trees. They were huge, powerful trees, hundreds of years old, towering high above the ground. Tucked between the mammoth trunks was a large clearing that was shaded by the canopy above.

As they walked closer, Kaladin could see that a large platform had been constructed in the clearing. It looked so natural amongst the trees that he had hardly noticed it. If he hadn't known better, he would have thought that the platform had simply *grown* there, rather than having been built.

A sitting area surrounded the platform. It too had been designed to fit in with the natural beauty of the forest. Here and there, holes had been cut in the floor of the wooden deck to accommodate younger trees as they reached toward the sky. Kaladin had never seen anything like it.

Sitting patiently, several of Lambec's inhabitants watched with interest as Kaladin and Tyban entered the clearing. Kaladin could feel their eyes upon him as he made his way through the sitting area. Tyban took a seat and motioned for Kaladin to sit next to him.

As the minutes passed, Kaladin's anticipation began to grow. He could literally feel the energy of this amazing place flowing through the trees, the platform, the others in the stands and through his own body.

"What are we waiting for, Tyban?" Kaladin whispered, breaking the silence.

"Shhh! You will soon see, Kaladin. Be patient," Tyban replied.

Kaladin did as he was told, trying not to be overwhelmed by his excitement. Men and women trickled into the clearing, filing into the stands, joining the silent gathering in the woods. Most wore a basic training uniform like Kaladin's. However, a few of the older warriors wore tan robes that, Kaladin imagined, signified their level of experience.

Soon the seats were all filled and the soft ringing of a metal chime filled the air. As the ringing faded, Tyban rose to his feet and slowly walked down to the platform.

"My brothers and sisters, fellow warriors, today we have a new face amongst us."

Eyes and heads turned to look at Kaladin. Some of the faces smiled softly, but most simply studied Kaladin with a curious interest. Kaladin nodded in nervous acknowledgement.

Tyban continued, "His name is Kaladin Lux and I have brought him before you so that we might see if he is ready to further his training with us along the path of the Enlightened Warrior." Tyban gestured for Kaladin to come forward and join him on the platform.

Kaladin swallowed hard and eased through the crowd to Tyban's side. Despite his nervous excitement, Kaladin could still feel warmth, a sense of security and safety that he had never experienced before. The faces of the warriors in the crowd were not those of competitors or potential enemies, but of friends and travelers on a similar path.

"Kaladin," Tyban said, "this is the time to show us what you have learned, a time for us to see if you are ready to travel further along this path, and a time for you to learn where your limits truly lie. Are you ready?"

Kaladin nodded to his companion and tried to center himself in preparation for what was to come.

"Very well, let us begin with weapons." Tyban nodded to a warrior seated in the first row. "Duras, if you please…"

A tall, lanky figure in the first row, Duras reached under his seat and removed a narrow canvas bag. With the bag tucked under his arm, he stepped onto the platform next to Kaladin. Tyban took his place in the stands next to the other warriors and watched intently.

Duras stood facing Kaladin and smiled as he opened the canvas bag. From the bag he produced four fighting sticks, each several feet long. He handed two of the sticks to Kaladin. Kaladin had used weapons such as these in the past; they had been a regular part of his training before he was banished from Thelius.

Following Duras' lead, Kaladin grasped a stick in each hand and stepped back a safe distance from his would-be opponent.

Still smiling, Duras ceremoniously saluted Kaladin and stood in a ready position. Kaladin returned the gesture and similarly took his position on guard.

"Begin!" called Tyban from his place in the front row.

With that, Duras and Kaladin began to circle around each other, twirling their sticks in rhythmic patterns back and forth. Like a delicate chess match, each was carefully studying the other, planning his move.

Suddenly, Duras lunged forward, swinging toward Kaladin's lead hand. Kaladin blocked just in time and engaged Duras with a series of attacks and counter-attacks. Not to be caught off guard, Duras returned the blows one-for-one to each of Kaladin's moves.

The whirling sticks, made of a light and flexible wood, banged against each other with a resounding "crack" as each fighter swung in a rapid-fire attack and defense. To the untrained eye, the match would appear to be a haphazard blur of sticks and bodies colliding clumsily with each other. To the warriors watching in the stands, though, this was a combative exchange of a high degree, each movement coordinated to that of the opponent.

Duras momentarily disengaged from Kaladin's attack and stepped back to measure his opponent. He circled around to Kaladin's side, smiling and studying the young warrior. This irritated Kaladin, who wanted to quickly end the match, proving himself to the warriors watching in the stands. Duras was playing and toying with Kaladin, though. Kaladin was being tested and he felt himself beginning to grow anxious.

With renewed vigor, Duras attacked anew. Kaladin managed to hold his ground, but Duras pressed him harder still. Flailing in dizzying spirals, their sticks struck against each other in rhythmic measure, beating out a drum-like cadence.

Kaladin could barely hold off the force of Duras' relentless attack. His hands struggled to grasp the sticks as they swung back and forth. His shoulders, straining under the pressure, were aching for release. Duras, though, seemed as fresh as when the match had begun.

Unexpectedly and without any warning, Duras snaked his lead arm around one of Kaladin's sticks and jerked it free, sending it tumbling across the platform. Duras shoved Kaladin in the chest, staggering him backward.

Frustrated and partially disarmed, Kaladin tried to compose himself. Duras, watching Kaladin's response, backed away and dropped one of his sticks to the ground.

Kaladin tried to shake off the fatigue in his arms as he prepared himself for another round. With only one stick, he would have to be much more careful.

Twirling his stick through the air, Duras stepped forward and swung down toward Kaladin's head. Instinctively, Kaladin raised his stick to deflect the blow while simultaneously covering with his empty hand. He countered quickly, swinging toward Duras' shoulder. The master warrior defended and countered in turn. Again, the two opponents engaged in an intricate exchange of blows and parries that looked more like a dance than a battle.

Kaladin and Duras were much closer this round, their feet shuffling ever so slightly as they repositioned themselves in response to each other. Not the wide swinging arcs of the last round, their sticks only seemed to tap together lightly as they made contact. However, both warriors knew that their stick was the only thing that stood between their opponent and a broken hand. A match of this kind required nothing less than the highest level of timing and precision.

Once again, Kaladin could feel frustration seeping back into his mind. Rather than focusing on the match itself, he was preoccupied with the outcome, with trying to win, trying to make an impression upon the warriors who watched intently from the stands. With each passing exchange between him and Duras, the tension grew, struggling to be set free.

Duras was no longer Kaladin's opponent. His enemy was his mind, turbulent and unbalanced. He struggled to gain control of the match, but the harder he tried, the more difficult it became. Finally, Duras capitalized upon Kaladin's lack of focus and effortlessly wrenched Kaladin's remaining stick from his hand and scooped it under his arm.

Kaladin sighed deeply and hung his head. He felt beaten and humiliated. Having obviously lost as he had, Kaladin wondered what would happen next.

"Well done, friend," Duras said with a great smile and extended his hand toward Kaladin. "You gave me my morning exercise."

Puzzled, Kaladin shook Duras' hand. "But, I lost," Kaladin replied.

"That you did," Duras said. "But not without skill. You have a fine technique and definite potential." He turned and nodded to Tyban.

Tyban nodded in return and gestured for Duras to return to his seat. The spectators in the crowd wore a mixture of curious smiles and knowing contentment upon their faces as Kaladin looked out, trying to judge their reaction to his performance.

"Kaladin," Tyban said, "how do you feel?"

Kaladin paused and took a deep breath. "Frustrated. I wanted to do better."

"Even a little angry, perhaps?" Tyban continued.

"Yes," Kaladin whispered softly.

"Focus your mind; put your attention on what is, Kaladin. The past, the future, they don't exist anywhere but inside your mind. Put your attention on the here and now, and draw your strength from it."

Kaladin nodded in agreement.

"Now, if you're ready, we'll continue," Tyban said.

Kaladin's eyes widened. *Did he say continue?* Kaladin asked himself. "You mean I'm not finished?"

"Far from it, Kaladin, far from it," Tyban said with a smile as he gestured to another warrior seated in the back of the stands...

By the end of the morning Kaladin had completed four more matches with the expert warriors of Lambec. Following the weapons were various rounds of kickboxing that pushed Kaladin's endurance and empty hand skills to their limit. Next followed close range infighting that tested his ability to "feel" his opponent's intentions through sensitivity and bodily awareness. Then came the grappling and ground fighting, which required a high level of both technical mastery and control. Finally were several rounds that integrated all of the fighting ranges together in a continuous flow. From long range through empty hands, to ground fighting, Kaladin was forced to blend it all together.

The matches tested Kaladin's skills unlike ever before. A few of the rounds ended with Kaladin as the victor, but most of them ended in defeat, which frustrated him deeply. His heart filled with doubt as to ever being accepted as a member of Lambec.

Following his final match, Kaladin was asked to wait on the platform while the members of the crowd convened to discuss his performance. The sweat dripped from his tired body as he anticipated their decision.

Tyban stepped up to Kaladin to offer encouragement while the others spoke amongst themselves. "You fought well today, Kaladin," Tyban said.

"I hardly won any of my matches," Kaladin replied in disgust.

"Fighting well doesn't always mean winning, you know," Tyban said.

"But how will they know what I can do if I can't show them?"

"Trust me, they know more than you imagine. Someday you'll understand." Tyban's tone was ominous, almost as if he could see into the future.

The crowd was beginning to return to their seats.

Kaladin's heart raced in his chest as one of the elderly warriors stood to face him and Tyban.

"Kaladin," the aged and kind voice filled the air, "today you have shown us that you are a warrior with great skill and promise. But the potential for what you might become still lies trapped within you. Only you can free it to blossom in this world.

"You imagine that we are here to pass judgment upon you and decide if we would have you join us. But in truth, you were welcome here from the moment you first arrived. If any judgment of worthiness or unworthiness exists, it is within you. The choice to stay and grow is not ours, but yours."

Kaladin's face brightened.

The old warrior continued. "What concerns us is not how well you fight, or what style you use, but rather *who it is* that is fighting. You have given us a glimpse of who you are, and with that knowledge we ask you to join us in order to further your training. Know, however, that it is not an easy path. You have great abilities and you have discovered much about the art of combat, but there is far more for you yet to learn."

Kaladin's tension had begun to fade and was replaced by the growing reverence he felt in his heart. He nodded solemnly, feeling the honor and privilege of being asked to join the warriors of Lambec.

"Each of us has our own challenge, and you are no different. It is what makes us who we are, unique and individual. However, facing that challenge will not be without struggle.

You must look deep within yourself to know what it is you must overcome. In doing so you will become who you truly are."

Kaladin nodded again, feeling strangely vulnerable before these insightful warriors. He knew there was something within holding him back, but he couldn't see it clearly yet.

Once more the aged warrior spoke. "All we can offer is guidance and support as you further your training. The real work will be yours and yours alone." There was a long pause before he spoke again. "What is your decision?"

Kaladin raised his bowed head and looked into the eyes of the warriors before him. This was what he had been searching for, and yet he was hesitant. He wondered whether he was up to the "challenge" the elder had mentioned. Would he be able to overcome those things that held him back? Would he fail?

A door had opened before Kaladin and he stood at the threshold. Despite his uncertainty, he knew he couldn't turn back. He had come too far. After everything he had learned, everything he had seen, the world would never be the same. Going forward was the only choice.

"I accept," Kaladin answered reverently.

"Excellent," the elder warrior said. "Welcome to Lambec, Kaladin. Welcome to your new home." With that, the chime rang once again and the crowd of warriors applauded their newest arrival.

Kaladin felt a warmth and acceptance he had never experienced before as he smiled at the onlookers. Filing down from their seats to the platform, the warriors greeted him with smiles and a flood of handshakes. There couldn't be a better place for him to be.

PART III

CHAPTER 13

Weeks and months passed as Kaladin began to settle into his new environment. His fellow warriors had welcomed him with open arms and hearts and were eager to help him learn and grow.

He regularly attended training sessions with warriors of differing backgrounds, exposing himself to new methods and ways of combat. Techniques he had never experienced were freely offered for his consideration and study. Warriors of varied styles and abilities displayed foreign and exotic forms of combat, amazing Kaladin with new ideas and concepts.

This wasn't the competitive, striving life that he had known in Thelius. Here were brothers and sisters who honored and respected each other. They weren't concerned with proving themselves to Kaladin, only in helping him grow. Demonstrating a new technique wasn't for the sake of showing off or a display of one's abilities. It was purely to illustrate the proper method or skill.

Training became an amazing exchange of knowledge between both the newest warriors and the most venerated veterans. When studying a particular technique, Kaladin was asked what he thought the most effective means for its delivery would be. His answers, rather than being judged as right or wrong, were given the utmost consideration and respect, so that all might understand another point of view. This was unheard of in Kaladin's experience. In Thelius, Kaladin couldn't express his views. He was made to follow the old tradition blindly, without question.

Kaladin looked forward to each day's training, knowing he would learn not only about combat, but about himself as well. He was starting to see how his preconceived beliefs and views were being challenged. He was becoming more aware of the mental "wall" that was the threshold to those things beyond his experience. And he would often have insights into the tendencies and habits that slowed down his progress.

For instance, with awareness, Kaladin could see that his habitual instinct to practice a technique with only his strong side forward was preventing him from creating a balanced relationship between his mind and body. By training both sides of his body equally, Kaladin opened himself up to new possibilities, and began to feel the harmonious nature of his entire being.

The concept of competition, like the other aspects of Kaladin's training, had taken on a new expression. Sparring matches were still a regular part of training, but now they were an exciting learning exercise that usually ended in laughter and insight, not bloodshed. This differed greatly from the sparring matches of Kaladin's past in Thelius, during which warriors were intimidated and beaten just to prove personal superiority. In Lambec, warriors trained to perfect themselves and in the process help each other learn. Such contrasts became the rule rather than the exception in this amazing place.

Each of the warriors had unique skills and abilities that contributed to an amazing and varied blend of martial arts that Kaladin was learning. One day he would learn knife fighting, another he was wrestling on the ground, the next cart-wheeling and somersaulting through the air. He was ever learning something new and exploring the seeming limitless possibilities of his body.

Kaladin relished this new and comprehensive training and every day he felt as if he were learning more than the day before. But despite his progress, a growing disquiet had begun to take root in the back of his mind. Something was not right and it tugged at his thoughts, just out of reach. In quiet moments of meditation his attention would often be drawn back to the frightful dream in which his evil counterpart mercilessly destroyed Valec. He struggled, trying to force himself to believe he had moved past those times, but the image haunted him still. Diving deeper into his training, Kaladin hoped that in time his dark visions would pass.

Kaladin loved every minute of his training, but equally fascinating were his lessons with Tyban. They would routinely walk along the shore or through the heavily wooded hills and discuss Kaladin's progress or the nature of the world in which they lived.

"Tyban, remember telling me about the levels of a warrior's development?" Kaladin asked one day while walking along the beach near the village.

"Yes I do. Why?"

"I'm curious. Does everyone go through these stages?"

"Sooner or later," Tyban replied. "Everyone will grow eventually. It's just a matter of time."

"But why does it take some so much longer than others? Take the warriors in Thelius. It doesn't seem like they're going anywhere. Here, on the other hand, I learn so much it sometimes makes my head hurt."

Tyban laughed. "Well, Kaladin, some of us choose to stay at a particular level because we think we have to, or we have so much fun there that we can't bear the thought of letting go. It all comes down to just how attached you've become to where you are." Tyban paused for a moment and bent down to pick an exquisitely colored stone from the sand. Specks of silver and blue shimmered on its surface in the afternoon sunlight.

"Take this stone," he continued. "This stone is like a phase in your development. It's unique, beautiful, and special to you. But if you choose to focus only on this stone, making it all-important, you aren't able to experience the rest of the universe. Similarly, if you get too attached to the scenery, you'll begin to identify with *it* instead of the one who is *seeing* it.

"So attachment is what holds us back from growing," Kaladin replied insightfully. "And in that attachment, we create limitations to keep us imprisoned at that level?"

"Yes." Tyban replied. "Think about it, Kaladin. Attachment is one of the primary ways in which we make ourselves suffer. We become attached to any number of things; friends, family, relationships, the past, our ideas of the future, our belongings, our sense of self. All of these things are natural and normal to experience, but the attachment to any one of them sets us up for pain and anguish when we no longer have them. Thus we spend huge amounts of time and energy trying to hold on to the objects of desire. Only through detached involvement are we able to accept the change and uncertainty of life and embrace life as it is, with openness and acceptance."

"But it can be hard to let go of those things we have grown attached to," Kaladin added.

"Indeed, Kaladin. But do you see how in attachment we hold ourselves back from growing? It is as if you are flowing down a river toward a beautiful ocean but instead of flowing with the current, you hold onto the riverbank, clinging to branches and stones along the way. Worse still, you might even try to fight the current and swim upstream. Deep down, life knows where it's taking you. The challenge is to have faith in your journey."

"But does that mean we should never stop along the path?" Kaladin asked.

"There really isn't any right or wrong answer, Kaladin. You are free to choose however you like. But the act of being *conscious* of those choices makes all the difference. In being aware of your choices, you choose those situations, those opportunities, those experiences that support your growth. Therefore, your growth becomes certain. It is without awareness that the process slows down."

"Like the warriors of my old city."

"Yes, unfortunately. But there is hope for them still."

"Then you think they will grow out of their limited beliefs?"

"Perhaps," Tyban said and tossed the brightly colored stone to Kaladin.

Snatching the pebble from the air, Kaladin rolled it around in his palm and noticed the intricate pattern of blue and silver. He nodded and smiled to Tyban in silent thanks and tucked the stone in his pocket.

CHAPTER 14

There's something I need to show you today, Kaladin," Tyban said.

Kaladin had been returning to his cabin after an early morning sparring session when his friend found him.

"Oh?" Kaladin was curious. Whenever Tyban wanted to teach a lesson or make a point, the experience would always be one to remember. The other warriors in Lambec were also fine teachers, but there was something about his friend that made Tyban's lessons all the more meaningful.

Cutting across the valley, Tyban led the way to the far corner of the settlement. The matted grass near the end of the valley marked the way warriors regularly walked on their way to the Great Temple. Kaladin, however, had never set foot inside the enormous building. He stared in wonder at the cathedral- like building as they walked up the carved stone steps to the massive doors. *Who could have built such an incredible structure?* he wondered to himself.

"This temple has been here for many generations," Tyban said, sensing Kaladin's awe. "The hands of many great warriors carved and carried the stones that make up its mighty walls. And each warrior who visits here, in turn, contributes a little bit of who they are as well."

Kaladin looked confused. "What do you mean, contributes a bit of who they are?"

Tyban paused in front of the great wooden doors. "Everything you think and feel affects the environment around you. You've already begun to have glimpses of this interconnectedness in your training. But the connection goes deeper than you realize."

"How so?" Kaladin asked.

"You and every other living being give off subtle impressions that are recorded in your surroundings. If you are aware enough, you can tune into those feelings, learn from them. But for now it is important just to understand that they exist."

"Why now?" Kaladin was fascinated.

"Because," Tyban replied, "when you enter this temple you will be carrying with you who you are and leaving a little of that behind within its walls. Thus it is important to be focused and centered upon the ideals that brought you here. You will feel what I'm talking about, trust me."

Kaladin nodded as Tyban pulled upon a heavy iron ring mounted to the door. With a deep groan, the door swayed open and they stepped inside.

The sunlight splashed across the marble floor as they walked into the atrium. Kaladin squinted, trying to make out the details of the great hall as Tyban closed the door with a thud. In contrast to the bright sunlight outside, the temple interior was much darker and it took a moment for Kaladin's eyes to become accustomed to the shadows. Once he could see clearly though, his jaw dropped as he beheld the incredible structure.

The interior of the temple was truly magnificent. Its walls seemed to stretch on forever in front of Kaladin, and towered one hundred feet up to the curved ceiling. Stone pillars, like those outside the temple, lined its interior, supporting the heavy arches and powerful buttresses. Soft, glowing candlelight flickered from alcoves cut into the walls, dimly illuminating the sides of the temple. Further forward, torches were mounted into the pillars and splashed an inviting orange hue over the stonework.

As amazing as the sight of the temple was to Kaladin, it couldn't compare to what he was feeling. From the moment he stepped within its walls he had felt a sensation unlike any he had ever known before: complete peace, total silence. Silence so deep it seemed to swallow up the very thoughts of his mind into a blanket of nothingness. The tension in his body dissolved, his mind stilled, and in that moment, there seemed to be no past or future, only an eternal moment of tranquility.

He wandered between the wooden benches that lined the floor of the temple, following Tyban's lead. The polished stone platform near the far end beckoned, drawing Kaladin's attention. On either side of the raised platform stood large statues of hooded figures, arms outstretched to the sides, seemingly offering the wisdom of the generations of warriors that had come before.

"Over here." Tyban's voice seemed faint as a whisper.

Kaladin imagined that an explosion couldn't disrupt the deep ocean of silence that dwelled within the temple walls.

Beckoning Kaladin to join him, Tyban stepped through an archway and into a small antechamber next to the platform. Kaladin followed and found himself in a small room lined by wooden pews on three sides. More candles, mounted along the walls, shone a soft light throughout the tiny chamber. The wooden pews were covered with thick red cushions and Kaladin took his seat on one next to Tyban.

"Tyban, this is incredible. I didn't know places like this existed," Kaladin whispered.

"Then you feel it?" Tyban asked.

"How could I not?" Kaladin responded. "It would be impossible to miss."

"Yes. This temple is a vast storehouse of spiritual energy, created by the warriors who came here to meditate and seek wisdom. After many generations, the very walls and stones themselves have become infused with that energy of transformation. It is a sacred place. It is where many of us come to meditate. You too, may come here when you wish to seek peace or guidance. All we ask is that you enter with reverence and silent respect for the path you have chosen."

"I understand," Kaladin replied. Kaladin reflected upon his past and the negativity he used to feel in Thelius and the Arena. He remembered how that negative energy seemed to seep right into his bones at times. Now, here in the temple, he felt the opposite extreme. This was so very different, so powerful.

"Now," Tyban continued, "I said I had something to show you."

Kaladin looked surprised. "But I thought *this* was what you were going to show me."

"Something more, Kaladin. I'm going to take you somewhere."

"Where?"

"Somewhere within yourself. Now relax, close your eyes and quiet your mind." Tyban folded his hands in his lap and closed his eyes.

Kaladin did as he was instructed. He felt a deep and penetrating relaxation wash over him as he began to meditate. Perhaps it was Tyban's presence, or perhaps it was the temple's powerful energy, but within moments Kaladin was in a state of profound silence. Usually it took some time to quiet the restless thoughts that would come and go during meditation.

However, any distractions to Kaladin's peace were instantly engulfed in the powerful stillness that enveloped him.

In this deep tranquility, Kaladin lost all notion of time and space. He no longer sensed his body and was oblivious to the duration of past, present or future.

Images danced before his mind's eye. Stars, whirling galaxies, planets, oceans, deserts, lush forests, faces of old friends and family merged together into a giant tapestry. The images were like an eternal kaleidoscope of all that had been, all that was, and all that would be. In the midst of this reverie, though, Kaladin had become aware of a point of light before him. Glowing blue-white and becoming larger, Kaladin realized that he was being pulled toward the light. Events and people from his life streamed by on all sides as Kaladin was drawn into the tunnel of light at a great speed.

Suddenly there was a blinding flash and the sensation of an abrupt stop as Kaladin found himself in his body. He was standing upon a vast sheet of glass, stretched out as far as he could see. All around him was a rich night sky, infinite and unbounded, shining with the light of thousands of stars. Below him, as well, the expansiveness of space stretched out forever.

Several feet before him stood Tyban, observing. He had obviously arrived before Kaladin and was studying his student's reaction.

Kaladin smiled, absorbed in the experience. Despite being unsure of where he was, he felt strangely comfortable in this place.

"Where are we, Tyban?" Kaladin asked.

"This," Tyban answered, stretching out his arms, "is the playground of your mind. It is the fertile field of your imagination, the prelude to everything you experience in your physical form."

Kaladin listened intently to his friend, still deeply absorbed in his mystical surroundings.

"Here you are free to create yourself however you choose, to rethink this environment in any shape you find acceptable, to summon tools, weapons, guidance and abilities you never imagined possible. It is a place that you may use to train your mind, the instrument and governor of your material body."

"But how do I do that?" Kaladin asked.

"With the power of your intention, Kaladin," Tyban answered. "The world is a blank canvas we paint in our minds. Create this mind field as you see fit, and then return to it often and it will begin to take root in your physical form as well."

"Are you saying that whatever I do here becomes real in the physical world?" Kaladin asked skeptically.

"What I'm telling you is that all physical transformations take place on a mental level before they can take on material expression. You have progressed to a point where the ability to reach this creative level is open to you. And it is here, deep within, that those powerful and profound changes may take place. What you do here, consistently and with time, will become a part of your waking reality. You physical body will be convinced that it can do all manner of things once you train your 'mental' body here. Give it a try."

"What should I do?" Kaladin asked.

"Simply have the intention to make a change and see what happens. In this place creation occurs at the speed of thought."

"Like what?" Kaladin said.

"This is *your* personal sanctuary, Kaladin. It's up to you. Perhaps a little...scenery?"

Kaladin smiled and paused for a moment. "How about a mountain or two?" he said, thinking aloud.

Without warning, the landscape of his mind shifted and the infinity of space was replaced by a horizon of snowcapped mountain peaks.

Kaladin's eyes widened, amazed at the speed at which the change took place. *And grass and a blue sky*, he thought to himself. The thought was hardly complete before the grass sprouted under his feet and spread out in great ripples extending to the mountains, a dark blue sky stretching out above.

"This is amazing, Tyban!" Kaladin exclaimed.

"Yes, it's a power you've always had within you, but *now* you can truly experience it fully." Tyban looked around and gave Kaladin a sardonic smile.

"What?" Kaladin said, noticing Tyban's expression.

"Oh, nothing, it's just a little...conventional, don't you think?"

"Oh...really?" Kaladin said, smirking back. "Well, how about...this?"

Instantly the sky turned a deeply streaked purple, two ringed planets hanging suspended from the heavens. The grass had turned to gray sand, the mountains, rolling dunes in the distance.

"Much better," Tyban said with a laugh. "But remember not to get too caught up in the scenery. The scenery may come and go as you please, but transforming *yourself* is the point."

"I think I understand," Kaladin said. "But if changes happen instantly here, why can't they happen just as fast in the real world?"

"Because here," Tyban said, "everything is made of thought. Thought is light, instantaneous, and can change in a moment. It is *pure* energy. The physical world though, is much denser. Matter is heavy and takes force and effort to bring about change. Here, though, the instruments of change are timing and finesse."

"But how can living a fantasy make changes in the physical world?" Kaladin asked.

"First, this is not a fantasy in the usual sense of a make-believe world. It is a real aspect of yourself, a mental expression of who you are and what you might become. It can become as real as you believe it to be.

"And second, your physical body is a projection of your mental body; beliefs about yourself, your personality, your self-image. When you make the changes at the mental level first, the physical changes become less difficult, and eventually effortless. It's similar to pushing a heavy wagon when you could use a horse to pull the wagon for you. Where the mind goes, the body will follow."

"But…" Kaladin tried to object.

Tyban interrupted. "Don't worry about *how* it happens as much as just *letting* it happen, Kaladin. In time you will see."

Kaladin nodded and managed to stifle his need to know all the answers.

"This is your time now, Kaladin. Create a place that is comfortable and familiar to you, in which you might practice and refine your skills." Tyban turned and began to walk away from Kaladin. "It's time I was on my way."

"You're leaving?" Kaladin asked.

"Yes. You continue from here alone. Only you can decide what shape your training will take from here." Tyban's image began to fade and grow transparent as he spoke.

"Thank you for showing me this, Tyban," Kaladin said, smiling.

"You are welcome, Kaladin. I'll see you soon." And Tyban faded from sight.

It was early evening when Kaladin emerged from his meditation. Sitting alone in the small antechamber, Tyban had long since gone. In the interim, though, Kaladin had been busy creating his mental training hall. A place of refuge and learning, Kaladin looked forward to the new abilities and possibilities that lie ahead.

As he rose to leave the chamber, Kaladin heard something bounce on the stone floor. Looking down, he realized the pebble Tyban had given him must have slipped from his pocket while he was meditating. Kneeling closer, Kaladin noticed something strange: the stone was changing color in his hand. No longer silver with blue sparkles, the pebble had transformed before his eyes until it was charcoal gray, highlighted by streaks of dark red that branched out like veins along its surface. *That's strange*, Kaladin thought to himself, and wondered what it could mean.

CHAPTER 15

As Kaladin practiced and refined his newfound visualization techniques, his training became more fulfilling and amazing than it had ever been before. He was learning and growing faster than he had imagined possible. Abilities and skills that were once impossible to conceive of were beginning to awaken within him, often unexpectedly. These "dormant potentialities," as Tyban had explained to Kaladin, were powers and faculties of mind and body that most people never developed, but would begin to surface as Kaladin's awareness expanded. His meditative sanctuary had become the fertile ground into which he could plant powerful intentions, sending ripples of transformation through every fiber of his being and apparently, out into the physical world.

Refined senses of touch, smell, hearing, taste and sight were some of the first changes he began to notice. Perceiving the world on a level unknown to him before, Kaladin could "feel" the world with much more sensitivity than he knew was possible. Colors, vibration, texture, fragrance, flavor; all had become enhanced, granting him a sharper experience of the world.

Speed, reflexes, timing and strength had also become more developed, not through physical exercise, but through the mental training and rehearsal Kaladin performed daily in his mind. These highly cultivated attributes allowed Kaladin to experience combat from a heightened perspective and granted him the ability to perceive his training opponents as if they were moving in slow motion. With this finely tuned perception, Kaladin could perform a counter-move before the opponent had completed his attack.

Even more amazing were the abilities that seemed to defy the very laws of nature Kaladin had accepted all his life. The law of gravity, which had always been so irrefutable, now seemed much more flexible. During acrobatic combinations, Kaladin felt strangely lighter than he had in the past, barely feeling his feet touching the ground. He could jump higher and perform incredible somersaults from the walls of the training hall and land perfectly, ready to launch into his next move.

With this ongoing practice Kaladin had begun to cultivate an intuitive sense beyond the limits of his rational mind. Transcending the physical, he was slowly learning how to stretch his perceptions beyond the limits of time and space. Flashes of knowledge and insight from times and places he had never visited seemed to spontaneously pop into his awareness, giving him guidance at just the right time, pointing him in just the right direction.

During his meditation one afternoon, Kaladin envisioned himself performing an exotic sword technique that he had never tried before, yet it felt so natural, so effortless, that it almost seemed as is it were performing itself through him. The technique was so compelling to Kaladin that during his sword training the next day the technique emerged at the perfect time to completely overwhelm Seedah, his elder, more experienced training partner.

"Where did you learn that technique, Kaladin?" Seedah asked.

"I don't really know," Kaladin replied. "It just came to me during my meditation yesterday."

"That is a very ancient technique; one that is rarely ever taught. It takes years of practice to master, yet you perform it as if you've known it all your life."

Kaladin felt slightly awkward but exhilarated at the same time. "What does it mean, Seedah?"

"I do not know, Kaladin. I will have to discuss it with Tyban."

છ

It was a week later that Kaladin's troubles began. Up until that point everything had been going perfectly. Kaladin couldn't have felt more at home and more fulfilled in his life at Lambec. It was the enlightened warrior's dream life, and Kaladin was living it. But despite the supportive atmosphere that Lambec provided, Kaladin had begun to feel anxious. A growing unrest was taking root in the back of Kaladin's mind, troubling his days and nights.

He knew he was becoming better; faster, stronger, more powerful than he had ever been. By channeling his mental powers, Kaladin realized that unbelievable abilities were clearly within his reach; it seemed as if there were no limits to his power.

However, with his growing skills came an unexpected partner: pride. Kaladin was starting to feel proud of himself, perhaps too proud at times, as if he were better than everyone else; that no one mattered but him. Supremely confident in his abilities, he knew his skills were surpassing those of most of the other warriors in Lambec. He had overheard some of them talking about him one day, commenting about his impressive abilities and how quickly he was growing, confirming what he already believed and strengthening his growing ego.

Kaladin hadn't expected these feelings and was confused about how to deal with them. Up until then he had been searching for answers, for the learning he felt his life had been leading him to. Now, after achieving a certain level of success, there grew a self-righteousness within that was dangerously close to becoming arrogance. He didn't like the feeling and secretly wished to return to the days of humility and wonder so common to his early training.

These feelings of egotistic self-importance became nearly overwhelming at times, and Kaladin struggled in an attempt to understand their origins and how to bring them under his control. He did his best to keep this side hidden from the other warriors and Tyban, fearing they wouldn't understand. The more he resisted, however, the greater his inner conflict became.

As he lay in bed in his cabin above the lake one night, Kaladin's mind darted through the perilous terrain that separated dream from nightmare.

He saw himself standing in the middle of the valley there in Lambec, the sky awash with purple and green, causing the surrounding trees to cast freakish and grotesque shadows over the hillside. The temple at the far end stood in ruins, a pile of rubble that was overgrown with moss and vines, long abandoned. Desolate and forgotten, Lambec was quiet as a tomb.

What had happened? Kaladin wondered to himself as a hot and stale wind swept through the valley.

"Don't you know?" came a hissing voice within his mind.

Kaladin turned to see a robed figure walking slowly toward him, his head draped with a dark hood. His walk was slow and deliberate with a powerful presence that made Kaladin uncomfortable.

"You must remember," the stranger continued. "After all, it was you who was responsible for all of this."

"Me? No…I couldn't have done this," Kaladin replied in terror.

"This and much more." The hooded figure stopped a few feet from Kaladin.

"Who are you?" Kaladin insisted.

The figure laughed. "Your ignorance amazes even me, foolish boy. See for yourself." The shadowy figure slowly pulled the hood back, exposing his face to Kaladin.

In silent horror, Kaladin stood frozen in fear as he stared into his own eyes. Older, darker, sinister, the face was a frightful image of his future self. Full of a shadowy corruption, this dark twin's face was tinted with a reddish-black color, his blue eyes penetrating deep into Kaladin's own.

"I am you, Kaladin. I am who you are meant to be, who you will become. Even now, you can feel me in your veins, reminding you of what you are." The hissing voice, raspy and heavy, made Kaladin's skin crawl.

"You…you are not me. You are not real. This is a dream," Kaladin replied, trying to stand his ground and hold onto what he believed to be true.

"Listen to yourself!" his counterpart shot back in a growl. "Remember what your 'master' Tyban has taught you; reality is created in your mind. Whatever we give power to becomes real. And your, our, waking life is no different. You have been giving power to me, and in so doing, I am real.

"Everything you have become is because of me," the shadow continued. "I have been the one behind all you have now and will have in the future. Without me you would have been dead long ago."

"No, no this can't be." Kaladin fought back. "I won't let it be." Struggling to come to terms with what he was hearing, Kaladin fortified his mind as best he could against his evil counterpart's verbal assault.

"Oh, brave words," came the shadow's mocking reply. "But you have no choice. You must face who you are. You have felt me growing stronger for months now. And I have grown tired of waiting. Now is the time to take the power that is truly yours and wield it."

"No. I won't." Kaladin dug himself in deeper and tried to hold his ground.

"Fool! I'm not reasoning with you, I'm telling you. You are not strong enough to resist."

In an unexpected and violent burst of raw power, the shadow figure delivered a lightning-fast backhand strike to Kaladin's jaw. The force of the blow, unlike any Kaladin had ever experienced, sent him hurling in an uncontrollable spin, arcing backwards several dozen feet. He thudded to the ground along the hillside of the valley, stunned and struggling to breathe. Lifting his head from the ground, Kaladin saw his counterpart walking slowly toward him, glaring intently.

Determined not to be caught off guard again, Kaladin forced himself to his feet, trying to shake off the pain in his jaw.

"You can't beat me, Kaladin. I know what you know, and more."

"We'll see," replied Kaladin in an obstinate tone. He swung hard at his opponent with his left hand and readied his right for an immediate follow-up, but there was no time. His shadow-self caught his attacking arm and jerked Kaladin forward into a devastating head-butt.

While struggling to keep his balance, Kaladin's legs were instantly swept out from under him by a brutal shin kick, leaving him crumpled on the ground. Bleeding and in tremendous pain, Kaladin looked through tearing eyes at his other self, towering over him.

"Don't you see?" the shadow jeered. "You can't beat me. None of them could beat me."

"Who...?" Kaladin's words choked out.

"Who do you think? Tyban and the others, of course, you idiot! Come, let me show you..." With that, the shadow scooped Kaladin up by the jacket of his uniform and hurled him toward the temple ruins. From one end of the valley to the other, Kaladin's body catapulted through the air like a shot until it reached the remains of the huge temple doors and slammed through them in an explosion of splintering wood and dust.

Following close behind, the shadow warrior picked up Kaladin's motionless body from the marble floor and dragged it into the crumpled remains of the temple mausoleum.

Holding him by the back of his uniform, the shadow pulled Kaladin up to his feet. Before them was what seemed to be an endless row of sarcophaguses stretching further than it seemed the temple walls could accommodate.

"They're all here, Kaladin. Look for yourself," said the shadow in smug satisfaction.

He held Kaladin before Duras' tomb, then Seedah's and, finally, he dropped his broken body before the tomb of his friend Tyban.

Kaladin raised his hand to touch the carved letters of Tyban's name. Kaladin managed a whisper. "You killed them...why?"

"Because they were weak, and foolish. They wanted to control me. But they couldn't."

"No. No, no. This can't be happening," Kaladin pleaded.

Kaladin could feel the energy draining from his body as he lay helpless on the floor. Beaten physically and emotionally his hand slipped from Tyban's sarcophagus. As he lapsed into unconsciousness, he could hear the shadow's voice echoing through his mind:

"There's no use fighting. You can't win. Soon you'll accept what you are. Then you'll see."

CHAPTER 16

Covered in sweat from his nightmare, Kaladin raced through Lambec. Dark morning clouds blanketed the sky, foreshadowing a coming storm. The images were still fresh in his mind as he searched through the settlement for his friend and teacher, Tyban. Kaladin didn't want to think about the nightmare, but it all seemed so real, so terrifying and clear in its meaning. No matter how he tried, he couldn't shake the horrible vision from his mind.

After what seemed like an eternity of searching, Kaladin found Tyban meditating alone in the temple garden. Relieved to see his friend alive, Kaladin steadied himself as he walked through the stone pillars and toward the bench where Tyban sat in silence.

"Something's wrong, Kaladin," Tyban said with his eyes still closed. He had sensed Kaladin's approach and could feel his student's tension when he entered the garden.

"Thank goodness I found you," Kaladin said, still trying to catch his breath. "I'm in trouble…a nightmare; I can't let it happen…you were all dead." Kaladin's words came out in a jumbled mish-mash of scattered thoughts and fears all running together.

"Kaladin," Tyban's tone was firm. "Sit down. Breathe."

Kaladin did as he was told. He felt his world begin to settle down a little in Tyban's presence.

"Now," Tyban said, "tell me what happened."

With a deep breath Kaladin began to describe the details of his dream. Tyban listened intently as his student elaborated on his vision and fears of the future. When he had finished Tyban closed his eyes and sighed deeply.

"You have met your Shadow side, Kaladin," Tyban said at last.

"But it was just a dream, right?" Kaladin asked agitatedly.

"Well, yes, that's right. But dreams can be messengers from deep within your self. They are a very real level of awareness and what they tell you shouldn't be taken lightly, especially now."

"You mean my Shadow is *real?*" Kaladin's eyes widened.

Tyban spoke slowly and deliberately. "Yes, Kaladin, he is real. He is your hidden self, the repressed, fearful and hidden side of your personality. All the things that you dislike about yourself are his qualities."

Hearing this, Kaladin leaned forward, holding his head in his hands.

"We all have a Shadow side, Kaladin. We all have parts of ourselves that we don't want to bring out into the open. For most people, the Shadow looms quietly in the background, whispering softly, subtly influencing, holding them back, and blanketing them in fear.

"For us, though, warriors and seekers of higher truths, the Shadow becomes much more of a tangible enemy."

Kaladin felt a sense of hopelessness washing over him. "Why is that?"

"Because as you gain more awareness, more power, your personality gets attached to that power. It tries to take responsibility for it all. The *self-image* buys into its own sense of importance and makes itself a god, free to do whatever it wishes."

Hearing this, Kaladin thought about his recent difficulties. "And that's what's happening to me?" he asked fearfully.

"Yes, I'm afraid so. Your Shadow is trying to come to the surface, to take control of who you are and what you will be. You've been holding these feelings back, repressing them, haven't you?"

Kaladin nodded solemnly.

"In doing so, the Shadow gains more power. He grows in the darkness, in the recesses of your mind. In holding it down, it just grows more and more powerful. Like holding a bucket upside down in the water, you can't push it down forever. Sooner or later it pops to the surface."

Tyban paused for a moment and then continued. "Remember when the elder spoke of the challenges you would face when you first arrived? This is the biggest one of all. Understanding, confronting and eventually overcoming your Shadow is what your path is calling you to do."

"Confront him? Overcome him? *Are you out of your mind?*" Kaladin shot back in shocked apprehension. "He nearly destroyed me last night. How am I supposed to confront him, let alone defeat him?" The thought was totally absurd.

"You must face him, Kaladin, sooner or later. The more you grow, the more you learn, the more powerful your Shadow becomes as well. And if you refuse to face him, that power could be used to serve darkness instead of light.

"Your Shadow was right about one thing, Kaladin: you are a powerful warrior, one whose enlightenment could help transform and heal the world.

Kaladin sighed deeply. "How can you say that? I feel like I'm stumbling into the darkness and about to loose myself forever."

"I say that because I have trained many warriors, but none have had the spark, the untapped potential that I feel in you."

"Seedah has spoken with me about some of the abilities that you have been developing. Such skills are very rare, even in the most evolved of the warriors here in Lambec. Only a very few experience these states of power, and you seem to be one of them. However, if you allow your Shadow to gain control of these abilities, the darkness and pain he would bring is beyond measure."

"But how can I do it?" Kaladin asked desperately.

"All that you need to face this challenge is within you. You have but to bring that strength, that *knowingness*, to the surface and out into the light. It will not be easy, but you *can* do it."

Kaladin looked around the beautiful garden, lush with colorful flowers, and felt the first sprinkles of the coming rain. "I…I can't do it, Tyban. I just can't."

Tyban softened a bit. "Kaladin, I'm sorry, but you can't turn back. You know that. Once a mind has begun to see through the eyes of truth, the path only takes you forward, difficult though it may be. If you choose not to face your Shadow or try to repress it, things will certainly become far worse. Ultimately, you will give him all your power. If that happens, then I fear your nightmare could literally become a reality."

Kaladin's brow tightened as he hung his head. "You don't know what you're asking, Tyban."

"Oh, yes I do, Kaladin," Tyban said as he rose to his feet and put his hand on Kaladin's shoulder. "The road you walk I once traveled myself." Tyban seemed lost in thought for a moment, but quickly came back to himself. "You are not the first to pass this way…nor will you be the last. Within your heart lies the strength to make the journey before you."

Tyban nodded at Kaladin and walked out of the garden into the valley.

Alone, unsure, and fearful of the future, Kaladin hung his head as a clap of thunder rolled through the sky overhead. The light drizzle became a steady pour that washed over Kaladin's hunched body, chilling him to the bone.

CHAPTER 17

Rays of morning sunlight peeked through the trees as Kaladin trained in quiet solitude on the sandy beach. His white knit uniform fluttered in the breeze while he whizzed through the air in a spontaneous burst of energy and focused attention. The movements were as fresh and natural as the sunrise itself. Kaladin had practiced these techniques hundreds of times in the past, but by keeping himself centered on each moment, his actions felt new and alive, as if he were performing them for the first time.

Although he was focusing his attention tightly on his body and its movements, Kaladin felt acutely aware of the world around him. He sensed the grains of sand under his feet, the filtered rays of sunlight against his face, the smell of the wildflowers on the hill. Yet these things didn't distract him from what he was doing. Instead, they complemented his actions and made him feel as if he was totally merging into the moment. Rather than being simply a part of the background, Kaladin felt his environment to be a part of him; distinct, but deeply connected to him at the same time.

In the days that followed his nightmare, Kaladin's mind had been deeply imprinted with the horrible vision of his future. Terrifying as it was, he had come to accept the challenge that awaited him. In that acceptance his training had taken on a sense of focused determination and clarity of purpose unlike any he had ever known. Each training session, each technique had become a challenge that forced Kaladin to train harder than ever before. He knew he had no time to lose if he was to be prepared for the confrontation with his Shadow. Like a man possessed, he pushed himself to the threshold of near physical and emotional exhaustion. Yet whenever he felt himself to be on the verge of a complete and total collapse, an untapped reserve of energy rose to the surface allowing him to press on against what felt like insurmountable odds.

Strangely, in the act of accepting his fate, the mental turbulence that had been plaguing Kaladin recently had receded. As his mind became set on what he had to do, the flood of uncontrolled thoughts had finally begun to subside. In coming face to face with the architect of his fear and anger, he had unlocked the mystery that had been troubling him for so long. Now, for the first time Kaladin knew what he was up against and what it all meant, but could he win?

Launching forward into yet another complex combination of movements, Kaladin noticed a small orange butterfly out of the corner of his eye. The delicate creature was floating around his shoulder in its own dance, riding on the breeze that Kaladin's motions had created. Spinning and whirling around his miniature playmate, Kaladin pushed himself faster as he launched into a rolling battle-punch. Suddenly, in mid-delivery, Kaladin heard and felt an earth-shaking boom, then total silence. Stunned, he looked around, but could see no source of the sound. The world was quiet, too quiet, he thought; that's when he saw it.

Looking toward the water, Kaladin was taken aback to see that the waves had stopped moving. They were held suspended in mid-wave: one wave just milliseconds away from hitting the shore, waiting.

He turned and looked over his shoulder and saw the sand he had kicked up during his attack held motionless in the air, several inches from the ground. His small butterfly training partner was frozen, its wings outstretched in mid-flap. Further down the beach, he could see the splash of a crashing wave held suspended, as if captured in a painting.

Just as the shock of all this was starting to fade, there was another loud boom, and things jolted back to normal. The wave splashed against the shore, the sand rained onto the ground, and the butterfly fluttered off toward a patch of flowers. Kaladin stood dumbfounded and in complete disbelief.

"What was that?" he asked himself as he tried to collect his senses. "Am I dreaming, or did time just stand still?"

"You weren't dreaming." It was Tyban's voice coming from the hill as he walked down toward Kaladin. "With all that racket, I doubt if *anyone* is still sleeping."

"Tyban! What was that? One moment I was training harder than ever, and the next moment everything just stopped and was frozen in time."

"It appears you were breaking through one of the remaining limitations you've been holding onto. How did it feel?"

"Well, strange at first, but after a moment or two, it started to feel much more...*incredible*. I was feeling *so* alive in my training, almost like I was everywhere *and* nowhere and then suddenly it was as if I was in-between moments in time, just watching it all."

"Whenever we shift our perspective, even just by a small amount, the whole of reality can look radically different. Wouldn't you agree?" Tyban replied.

"Yes, it does," Kaladin said, still in a state of mild shock. "But how does it happen? How does any of this happen?"

Tyban paused. "When your spirit begins to dwell in the eternal present that is your *true essence*, through deep meditation and focused awareness, your mind and body transform to become an expression of that experience, and become capable of far more than what most people would imagine is possible."

"So you're telling me that my body and its abilities are a direct result of my level of consciousness?" Kaladin asked.

"Yes. And the more you experience that deep one-ness, the greater the transformation of your body and mind, right down to the very fiber of your being.

"And just now, you were feeling such an intense connection to the world during your training, that you may have had a faint intention to experience the timelessness of the present moment. That intelligence organized the outcome without your conscious thought. And without warning, you managed to hold your attention between *the past* and *the future*, and into the eternity of a single moment."

"So it was just an accident?"

"Not really; more of a *controlled* accident. As time goes on and you become more comfortable with the process, you'll be able to create whatever outcome you find to be appropriate. Give it some time."

Kaladin suddenly looked troubled.

"What's wrong?" Tyban asked.

"It doesn't seem like time is on my side anymore, Tyban. It feels like the Shadow is just waiting, hoping for the chance to gain more abilities and strength that it can use against me, against us all."

"Yes, you are right," Tyban said with a sigh. Your Shadow *is* waiting, biding its time. That's what it does. Remember, the longer you wait to face it, the more powerful it becomes."

"But I have to train. I have to be prepared. I'm not ready, Tyban."

Tyban's tone grew deadly serious. "Kaladin, listen to what you are saying. As long as you tell yourself that you're not prepared to face your Shadow, then you *never* will be. You are as prepared as you believe yourself to be." He paused. "Haven't you seen it yet, Kaladin?"

"Seen what?"

"That from the very beginning, your whole journey has been dictated by *what you believe*. Your beliefs structure everything in your experience. Restricted beliefs have limiting results. Unbounded beliefs have limitless possibilities. Your conditioning, the way you have taught yourself to think about the world and your reality, is what determines what you are capable of."

Kaladin turned to look out to the rolling waves on the lake. "I hear what you're saying, Tyban, I do. But why can't I feel it and *know it* fully? What am I missing? What more can I do?"

"That's just it, Kaladin. There's nothing more you *can do*.

Kaladin turned to stare at Tyban. "But, I…"

"Kaladin, all along you have been seeing this whole process, your journey, as one of *increase* rather than *decrease*."

"What do you mean?" Kaladin said with a bewildered look.

"Becoming an enlightened warrior, Kaladin, is not about the *accumulation* of new knowledge or techniques. Instead it is the process of *removing* all that is inessential to who you really are, the removal of all the inefficient, antiquated, heavy, cumbersome, useless ways of fighting; the useless *ways of being*. In doing so you see what and who you really are. Like the skins of an onion, you peel away everything that you don't need, until, in the end you find your essence in emptiness; the true *seed* of your being, from where everything is possible."

Kaladin's eyes suddenly widened. Something about what Tyban said struck a chord deep within his heart. In a flash he could see that all along he had been searching for answers outside of himself. Another technique, a new skill, an elusive insight, he *had* been accumulating so much, and yet he wasn't ever satisfied.

"You're right, Tyban," Kaladin said at last. He sighed deeply. "I understand." There was a long pause. "But what now?"

"You must trust, Kaladin. You must find a way to let go and believe that the power isn't something that comes from outside of you. It's not something that you can collect or accumulate more of, rather it is within you; it *is* you and has been there all along. In that emptiness lies the potential for all you will ever need. Now is the point where you must take a leap of faith and step confidently into the unknown."

"Have faith in the unknown? That sounds like a paradox. How does one do that?"

"There is no 'how' to do it, Kaladin. You must simply *take that step*. Faith means believing in something *unconditionally*. Not based upon the proof of your senses, but upon the trust of your heart and the knower within."

"Then, when I believe I'm ready...I will be." Kaladin nodded in understanding and turned back to the softly rocking waves.

"Exactly!" Tyban put his hand on Kaladin's shoulder as he turned to leave. "As you think, so shall you believe. And as you believe, so shall you become."

The sound of Tyban's footsteps faded into the distance as Kaladin knelt down on the sandy shore. Staring out at the distant horizon, he thought about what his friend had said and let his mind go inward. The world spiraled itself around Kaladin in a hazy blur of thoughts and emotions. "Step into the unknown," he whispered as he lost himself in the rhythm of the rolling waves.

CHAPTER 18

The soft moonlight bounced gently upon the lake's surface, its reflection twinkling over both the sand and Kaladin's pensive face. The entire day had come and gone, yet Kaladin remained unmoved. Seated cross-legged in the darkness, he stared out into the great lake, his gaze firmly fixed on the horizon. No longer seeking answers, Kaladin had let go of all of his expectations and fears, surrendering completely.

Throughout the day and night he had witnessed his thoughts in their coming and going but had refused to let them take control of his mind. His whole life had passed before his eyes as if it were a dream. But rather than being a participant in the dream, Kaladin was a removed observer, as if it were someone else's life he was watching. He witnessed without judgment all the choices he had made through his life, and how they influenced who he had become.

In this detached state, Kaladin's mind had given up its clinging to who he had imagined himself to be. Like a snake shedding its skin, those things with which he had identified himself began to fall away. His name, his body, his thoughts and emotions, his history, all those aspects of personality he had clung to could no longer define *who he was*. Beneath those changeable, impermanent concepts stirred something far greater and far more powerful than he ever imagined...his true self.

As this unexpected insight flooded upon him, a rush of energy shot up Kaladin's spine. Something incredible was happening. His hands and arms began to tingle, he felt an indescribable lightness in his limbs, and his entire body seemed as if it was expanding beneath his skin. A feeling of intense buoyancy washed over him and without warning, Kaladin's body lifted several inches off the sand and hung suspended in the air. As incredible as it was, this sensation stood in the background of Kaladin's mind. He maintained his focus and resolved to allow nothing to disturb his centered awareness.

Kaladin's mind and body were suddenly filled with not a thought, not a belief, but with a *knowing*. It was a distinct feeling, *knowing* beyond words or ideas, a knowing of who and what he was. Unclouded by all past ideas of what it meant to be a warrior, Kaladin's mind seemed to extend throughout the entire universe. An instant later, though, that cosmic awareness collapsed back into the single point of attention that was his body. As quickly as it had begun, the strange sensation ceased and his body came to rest on the beach once more.

The whole experience shook Kaladin with a jolt. His gaze, which had been so deeply rooted upon the dark horizon, returned to normal as he looked around the quiet, dark beach. Somehow, deep within, he had changed. The time had come.

 C820

A few scattered torches lit the pathway as Kaladin made his way back toward the village. The full moon painted Lambec with an eerie, otherworldly blue glow. The night air was cool and crisp against Kaladin's face, but he hardly noticed. His mind was focused on the task before him and he had never felt such determination, such clarity of purpose.

Descending into the valley on his way to the Great Temple, Kaladin noticed something strange happening a few hundred feet away in the center of the valley. There, a swirling stream of glowing red haze was forming just a few feet off the ground. Like a lazy tornado, the haze was spiraling inward on itself in a circular motion. With each step Kaladin took though, the vortex seemed to spin faster and faster, pulling in the surrounding air.

The wind began to whip through the valley in fierce gusts as the energy churned with growing intensity. Kaladin paused, knowing that what he was seeing could only mean one thing... his Shadow.

Then, almost as if on cue, the spinning cloud collapsed in upon itself in a burst of energy that shook the very ground Kaladin stood upon. A shockwave of expanding red energy blasted out from the center of the valley, washing over Kaladin and the entire village. When it had passed, Kaladin looked around to see Lambec in ruins, as it had been in his nightmare. Apart from a low otherworldly groaning sound, the village looked and felt lifeless as a grave.

Unaffected, Kaladin focused his gaze upon the center of the valley, where he could make out the silhouette of a kneeling figure draped in dark robes. The figure sat staring at Kaladin, his eerie blue eyes sinister and unemotional.

A reddish-black glow radiated from the Shadow as it had before, rippling out several inches around its body. Its face had changed, though. More disturbing and vicious than in the past, it bore little resemblance to Kaladin.

"So, you believe you're ready to face me now," the Shadow calmly snarled. "What has that old fool Tyban told you, that you can defeat me?"

"No," Kaladin replied as he slowly walked closer. "He only told me to know who I am."

"Good. Then you've *accepted* who you truly are," the Shadow sneered, supremely confident in himself.

"Yes I have." Kaladin said calmly with a deep resolve. "But it will never be you."

"You're more foolish than I expected. It will make no difference, though." His tone reeked of arrogance and self-importance. "You've already tasted what I am capable of."

"Things have changed. You won't rebuild your palace again." Kaladin stood firm as a mountain, his eyes deeply set on the kneeling figure before him.

"But you live in that palace, without it you are nothing. Without it you cannot survive."

"I have seen beyond your illusions. It is you who cannot survive without me. I am pure being, limitless expression of a self far greater than you can ever know. You would make me wear your mask and do your bidding out of fear."

Except for the hissing of his breath, the Shadow was silent. Clenching his fists, he lowered his gaze, glaring straight ahead.

"So be it," the Shadow replied. With that, he stretched out his arm and pressed his palm flat to the ground. The earth rippled under his touch as tendrils of red and black energy streaked out from his fingers. The energy darted underground only to re-emerge with an explosive burst of force. Growling from deep underground, huge wooden beams erupted through the floor of the valley and began to slowly ascend several feet into the air.

Kaladin watched without emotion as a large fighting platform assembled itself around he and his Shadow. Beams, rafters and columns materialized spontaneously and instantly from nothingness. A matted floor rippled out and covered the raised platform as racks of weapons appeared on either end of the ring. Dark wooden timbers formed the railing of the platform while thick columns supported the heavy rafters overhead.

Within moments, the structure was complete. Kaladin stood at one end while the Shadow knelt at the other. Unmoved by the Shadow's grandiose display of power, Kaladin stared at his enemy and spoke dryly, "More illusions."

Hearing this, the Shadow suddenly growled like an enraged animal and sprang to his feet. In one smooth motion, he turned to Kaladin, a bow and arrow materializing in its hands. Shadowy fingertips jerked free, firing the missile at its target.

The arrow whizzed toward Kaladin, cutting through the air like a knife. Kaladin twisted sharply to the left just as the arrowhead would've pierced his chest. It skimmed past his body, thudding to a halt as it buried itself into a heavy wooden beam.

Kaladin turned to face the dark warrior before him. The bow was still in his hands, but as he glared at Kaladin, he stretched the curved wood out before him, transforming it into a long staff.

Kaladin readied himself as the Shadow raised the staff and swung in a wide arc. He shuffled backwards and evaded the blow, feeling a breeze from the staff against his face. The Shadow closed the gap and swung again, just missing Kaladin's head.

Kaladin continued to evade the attack by backing up toward the platform's railing, but could feel that he would soon be out of room. With the Shadow's next strike, however, Kaladin flipped backward to land momentarily on the top beam of the railing and then instantly launched himself into a forward somersault that carried him over his opponent. He landed back-to-back with the Shadow and reflexively delivered a brutal elbow strike to the back of the Shadow's head.

Dropping the staff and sprawling forward, the Shadow staggered against the wooden railing. Momentarily stunned, he steadied himself, paused and defiantly twisted his neck with a cracking sound.

Squaring off against each other, Kaladin and his Shadow stared deeply into each other's eyes. With a slight smile, the Shadow nodded at Kaladin before lunging into a barrage of punches and kicks. Kaladin countered and returned with his own attack. The exchange continued for what seemed like a timeless eternity, neither opponent connecting with the other as they traded blows; so evenly matched were they in their skills.

Suddenly seeing an opportunity, the Shadow leapt across the matted floor, scooped up the fallen long staff and swung it heavily towards Kaladin. As it was about to connect, Kaladin caught the staff with his left hand and spun around to lock eyes with the Shadow once again. The two warriors froze briefly before struggling to overpower the other for control of the weapon. Without warning, the Shadow twisted his hip and struck the shaft with his elbow, breaking it in two.

The Shadow attacked again, swinging his half of the staff toward Kaladin. Reflexively, Kaladin blocked with his stick, covering his head from the oncoming blow, but as the two sticks collided, the Shadow saw an opening and delivered a rib-cracking palm-strike to Kaladin's stomach with his free hand. The blow hit Kaladin like dynamite sending his weapon tumbling to the floor and hurling him backward at least a dozen feet. He landed face down, stunned and gasping for air.

The Shadow strode toward his downed adversary glaring intently, the knuckles of his hands cracking in tight fists. To the Shadow's surprise, though, Kaladin had managed to rise to his feet and adopt a ready position against his foe. Kaladin wasn't about to give up, despite his aching chest and the taste of blood in his mouth.

"Destroying you is something I'm going to enjoy," the Shadow said as he tossed his stick to the mat.

Kaladin didn't reply. He simply held his stance and gazed at his opponent. Whatever the outcome, he knew there was no other way.

The Shadow lunged forward, unleashing a salvo of punches. Kaladin tried to block as best he could, but he found himself overpowered by the Shadow. Several blows connected to both his face and body, sending him to the ground once more.

Despite being knocked down, Kaladin managed to swing his leg into the heel of the Shadow's foot, sweeping his leg and sending him sprawling onto the mat next to Kaladin.

Recovering quickly, the Shadow sprung into the air, spun his body directly over Kaladin and prepared to land with a devastating punch to the chest of his opponent.

Pivoting his body just in time, Kaladin spun out of the way as the Shadow's fist slammed into the mat, cracking the wood beneath. Kaladin seized the opportunity and yanked the Shadow off balance and onto his back. With a mighty thud, Kaladin landed directly on top of the Shadow and began to unleash an avalanche of punches to his foe's face and body.

In this position, the Shadow was trapped and the more he struggled, the more helpless he became. Punches hailed down from Kaladin with unstoppable force. The end seemed near, when suddenly, in the midst of unceasing punches, the Shadow spoke.

"Yessss," hissed the sinister voice.

Kaladin paused for a moment in his attack, his fist cocked by his ear.

"Does this feel familiar?" The Shadow spoke in a slow, deliberate tone.

Caught unprepared, Kaladin flashed back to his fight with

Valec a lifetime ago. He saw himself planted atop his crippled opponent's chest, ready to deliver the fatal blow.

"You can't fight who you are, Kaladin. Look at yourself!"

Kaladin paused and looked at his raised fist. To his sheer terror, he saw streaks of crimson and black spreading through his fingertips, climbing up his wrist and arm.

"You are becoming me. Finish it now and we will become one!"

"No," Kaladin gasped to himself.

"Yes!" the Shadow snarled. In a burst of reclaimed power, the Shadow sat upright, grabbed Kaladin's tunic and head-butted his foe with enough force to hurl him backward and onto the ground.

The Shadow popped back to his feet and stared at Kaladin with a sinister smirk, clearly pleased with himself.

Staggering to his feet, Kaladin looked down at his left hand. With a focused intent, he stared at his fingertips and composed himself. Within seconds the crimson-black streaks began to reverse their direction until they trickled out of his fingers and dissolved into nothingness. Back to their normal color, Kaladin flexed his fingers and locked his eyes upon the Shadow once more.

In a state of enraged shock, the Shadow flew into the air and shot forward toward Kaladin with an animal-like growl. The punch hit Kaladin like a cannon, sending him sprawling several dozen feet backward. Amazingly, he was able to rise back to his feet as the Shadow came at him once more.

Grabbing the front of Kaladin's uniform, the Shadow swung the body of his challenger into one of the vertical beams running along the edge of the platform. The heavy wood cracked and splintered as Kaladin's back pounded up against it. Another beam, and yet another gave way, as Kaladin was slammed like a rag doll into the huge supports. Finally, with a powerful punch, the Shadow knocked Kaladin across the training platform and into a rack of weapons. Crumbling under the impact, the rack sent sticks, knives, and swords scattering everywhere.

Dazed and fighting off waves of pain, Kaladin struggled for breath as the Shadow stood over him in apparent victory.

"Once you're gone, only I will remain," the Shadow sneered. "Without your resistance, there will be nothing that can stand in the way of my superiority."

The Shadow bent down to pick up one of the long swords that had been scattered upon the floor. He nonchalantly pulled the shining blade from its scabbard and gripped the hilt firmly in his hands, eyeing the curved metal. With a kick, he rolled Kaladin over onto his back and pinned his beaten rival down squarely with his right foot.

Somehow, amidst the blur of pain, something the Shadow said stuck in Kaladin's mind. "Without my resistance nothing will stand in the way," he said to himself.

Kaladin's mind whirled through a moment that stretched out like an eternity before him. All along he had been fighting his Shadow side, resisting it. Now, an incredible realization flooded over Kaladin; in resisting his Shadow, he had been giving it power! In the very act of struggling so hard against the Shadow, he had created the ground for the very conflict he found himself trapped in.

"Let go," Kaladin said to himself, feeling a profound transformation taking place.

Looking upwards, Kaladin watched as the Shadow prepared to thrust the sword downward into his chest. With the sword poised high in the air for a final blow, Kaladin's eyes met those of his dark self and spoke with a newfound calmness:

"Your existence depends upon the attention I give to you. The power is mine, *not* yours."

Enraged by Kaladin's comment, the Shadow snarled deeply from his throat and drove the blade downward with all his might.

Just at the moment when the steel should have pierced his chest, there was a burst of brilliant white light and Kaladin's body disintegrated into nothingness. The sword blade, under the Shadow's weight, buried itself into the floor of the platform, sticking fast.

The Shadow looked around the platform in a state of frenzied confusion, but Kaladin was not to be seen. Yanking the sword free, he kicked the pile of wooden rubble at his feet in rage.

"Over here." Kaladin's voice rippled calmly through the training hall. He had re-materialized several feet away, apparently healed of his injuries.

Spinning around the Shadow readied his sword to attack once again. In response, Kaladin extended his right arm, palm open. Without warning, another sword flew across the platform and into Kaladin's waiting hand. He drew it across his body in a slow, deliberate motion, taking a ready stance against his visibly surprised Shadow-self.

"Now..." Kaladin whispered, extending his sword toward the Shadow in an open invitation to attack.

Responding to Kaladin's gesture, the Shadow launched into an aggressive attack and the two warriors locked blades in a sword battle unlike any known before.

Metal flashed as it cut through the air, the blades swinging in wide powerful arcs toward their targets. Kaladin countered each of the Shadow's attacks effortlessly as the dark warrior struggled to regain control of the battle. The Shadow was attacking relentlessly in an attempt to overpower Kaladin with sheer force. It was of little use, though. The harder the Shadow struggled, the more difficult it became to out-maneuver his opponent.

Kaladin parried each slash and thrust the Shadow made with a minimum amount of effort. Each successive movement became more natural and spontaneous until suddenly, with a perfect delivery that seemed to happen all of itself, Kaladin's sword snaked itself around the Shadow's weapon as he simultaneously delivered a front kick to the Shadow's stomach. The Shadow tumbled backward under the force of the blow, his weapon bouncing clumsily across the mat next to him.

Desperately, the Shadow rose to his feet, reached for his weapon and hurled it at Kaladin. The blade spun through the air at an incredible speed, but Kaladin dodged easily and the sword harmlessly imbedded itself in the wooden railing behind him.

In a deliberate act of confident control, Kaladin stretched out his arm and opened his hand, allowing his sword to drop to the ground. With the odds evenly matched once more, Kaladin assumed his fighting stance for what he knew would be the final round.

With his attempts to destroy Kaladin falling short again and again, the Shadow rushed forward in a mad rage. The Shadow attacked with every combination imaginable, punching and kicking wildly. Despite the ferocity of the attack, it had virtually no effect upon Kaladin, who was dancing out of harm's way with unparalleled ease.

Then, in a moment of unbendable intention, Kaladin rushed his opponent with his own attack. He pounded past the Shadow's defenses effortlessly, harnessing the battle-punch that he had used so often in the past. But this time, he was focused, centered, and completely present in the moment. There was no anger, rage or fear; only stillness. The stillness was so profound that Kaladin almost didn't even notice the *boom* that shook through the training hall as he slipped into the timelessness of the moment.

Kaladin moved so quickly that the Shadow might as well have been a statue. He stood frozen in time as Kaladin flashed from side to side and riddled the Shadow's body with blow after blow.

Finally, after delivering a multitude of attacks, Kaladin's consciousness dropped back into the flow of time and he delivered the finishing blow by hurling his dark adversary into the air. Two dozen feet above the platform, the Shadow's body tumbled through space, smashing through three of the ceiling rafters before crashing down to the floor.

The crushed Shadow lay still at the far end of the platform. Kaladin stood over the body of his beaten counterpart with a placid expression upon his face. The Shadow stirred, and with a strained effort rose to its feet. Cuts and tears in the Shadow's tunic exposed where Kaladin's sword had found its mark as the dark warrior's strength began to fade. He wobbled, fighting to keep his balance, and looked into Kaladin's eyes with a confused expression.

"How…?" the Shadow asked.

Kaladin stared deeply at his foe. "I gave power to an illusion and you became real. In taking that power back, you do not exist."

The Shadow lifted his gaze as if he understood what Kaladin said. The Shadow, with the last of his strength, screamed in final defiance, "Noooooo!" The deep, dark glow that surrounded his form shimmered in a intense surge of crimson energy and then slowly collapsed into his body

As Kaladin watched, the Shadow's form began to dissolve. Streaks of crimson darted across its surface, peeling away layer after layer of the Shadow's spectral body. In another moment, it had disintegrated completely.

Kaladin looked around the wreckage of the training platform. Taking a deep breath, he slowly closed his eyes and composed himself. A deep sense of relief washed over him as a soft growing energy began to radiate from the core of his being. Suddenly, with an enormous flood of power, the sensation erupted from within his body, rippling out into the surrounding environment.

When Kaladin opened his eyes, the morning sunlight was softly shining on his face. The fighting platform had disappeared, and Lambec had been transformed back to the place he knew and loved.

Reaching into his pocket, Kaladin felt the small stone he had left there. Examining it closely, he was surprised to see that the black and red streaks had transformed into a pure silver surface, reflecting the world with perfect clarity. Kaladin smiled with understanding as he tossed the pebble in the air and walked up out of the valley. It would be a beautiful day.

PART IV

CHAPTER 19

A profound change had come over Kaladin in the months following the battle with his Shadow-side. He had grown both as a martial artist and as a human being. Walking through the dark forest of his fears had given him the confidence to know that there was no challenge he couldn't face. He felt above no one, beneath no one, and was independent of the approval of others. He was secure, not in any outside possession or ability, but in his knowledge of himself as a limitless expression of spirit.

As time wore on, Kaladin found himself doing more of the talking during his regular walks with Tyban. Tyban was always asking questions. Whether about a particular technique, the practice of meditation, or the experience of life as a whole, Tyban's probing always helped Kaladin look beyond appearances and see a deeper, larger vision of the way of the warrior. In the process, Kaladin often answered most of his own questions and grew to understand that Tyban wasn't teaching something new, he was simply helping Kaladin remember what he had always known.

One day, while they were sitting in the amphitheater together, Tyban turned to Kaladin and said, "Kaladin, what do you think the true purpose of studying the martial arts is?"

"Well, the purpose of study depends on *who* it is that is studying it," Kaladin replied.

"Go on."

"Specifically, the purpose would be dictated by the student's level of development or evolution. At a lower level of development, the purpose of training may be to learn to survive, to simply insure the continuation of a way of life. But that purpose would change as the warrior grew and changed, that is, *if* they chose to grow and change.

"At a higher level of evolution the purpose may be to create a new technique or philosophy, or means of self-expression."

"What is *your* purpose in training then, Kaladin? Where do you think this has all been leading?"

Kaladin paused for a moment, reflecting on how the reasons for his training had changed over time. He remembered how he had once fought merely to survive and to win someone else's approval. That was the way of the fighting Arena. But he had grown to value the life and well-being of others above his own ego's needs. He no longer felt any desire to harm others for personal gain of any kind. Kaladin had begun to strive for balance, harmony and peace. Paradoxically, despite the often vicious nature of the martial arts, Kaladin's training had cultivated a growing sense of non-violence and serenity.

He had continued to create his own unique expression of fighting skill. Rather than a style limited to any one particular discipline or form, Kaladin's style was a formless form, able to adapt itself to whatever conditions or situations presented themselves. Open to all techniques and concepts, but limited by none, his personal art was the expression of truth in combat. And through the expansion of his mind, Kaladin continued to break through the boundaries of space, time, and the physical world.

"It's changed so much over time, Tyban. I don't think it's about *fighting* anymore. I think it's about *me*. I'm training to learn who I am. That's what the martial arts are about, self-discovery. Other reasons may come and go, but self-understanding is where the truth in combat lies.

"The development of a martial artist is relative to his or her level of understanding. We're all striving to understand ourselves, but from different perspectives. So where one finds himself along the path determines the most appropriate response for their growth."

"And when you have all those perspectives?" Tyban asked.

"You have limitless possibilities. You can choose to act from whatever level you find to be appropriate."

Tyban was silent as Kaladin reflected on what he had said.

"But what if I don't want to fight at all, Tyban?"

"You won't have to. At that level of development it simply becomes impossible for others to experience hostility in your presence."

"Because they're afraid?"

"No, because the level of *your consciousness* literally changes the surrounding environment. When that happens, it becomes impossible for an individual to become a potential opponent; they simply won't have the desire to fight. And from that point of view, fighting becomes a means to learn how *not* to fight."

"Self-perfection through the vehicle of self-protection," Kaladin said.

Tyban smiled, nodding his head in quiet agreement.

"Perhaps I'll reach that level someday."

"You are closer than you think, my friend," Tyban replied. "Closer than you think."

CHAPTER 20

Kaladin sat on a high grassy overlook, immersed in deep meditation. The waves far below had long since faded to the softest whisper in his consciousness. The sun was close to setting and its warmth was barely noticeable. Far above, in the branches of a large tree, the breeze gently swirled through the leaves as if they were feathers. In his silence, though, Kaladin had drifted into an even more profound and peaceful landscape, one where all the boundaries between this and that, right and wrong, near and far, no longer existed. He had slipped into the experience of timeless and formless being beyond all distinctions.

Just a slight trickle of thoughts would float through his consciousness from time to time. Then they would be gone, leaving the silence once more. It was during one of these moments of activity that Kaladin thought of his family in the city he had left behind. He wished he could see them, to know that they were well, but then the silence swallowed up his thoughts into the stillness once again.

Suddenly, a surge of energy rushed through Kaladin's body and interrupted the silence. He opened his eyes, and to his amazement, he was standing in the Center Square of the city he had left behind long ago. Night was falling and he could hear the shouts of the spectators in the Arena nearby.

"What's happened?" Kaladin wondered aloud. He paused to collect his thoughts. Then it became clear. *My thoughts were of this place,* he thought to himself. *I had the desire to be here and it just happened, without me even trying.*

He smiled to himself as he looked around. Everything seemed as it was when he left. *My family! They were the reason I was thinking of the city.* His mind was filled with images of his parents and brother. He imagined that they must be at the Arena, watching the nightly fights. With that thought, he felt another rush of energy, a blur of motion filled his eyes, and there he was, seated in the stands of the Arena itself. Again, Kaladin was momentarily stupefied, but this time he quickly shook off the disorientation, realizing that here, amongst all the people, he would easily be recognized.

Oddly enough, he didn't seem to be noticed. The two women he was seated between talked amongst themselves as if he didn't exist. When one woman reached over to touch the other, Kaladin noticed that her hand passed right through his left arm as if it weren't even there. Kaladin suddenly realized that this couldn't be his physical body. It had to be a projection of his consciousness from the hilltop in Lambec.

The roars of the crowd pulled Kaladin's attention to the action in the ring below. A young man was in the midst of a running tackle against his much larger opponent. Just as he was about to take his victim to the ground a loud gong rang throughout the Arena. The fighters disengaged from each other and stood to face the city elders.

"Orin Baluk!" An elder's voice boomed over the fading din of the crowd. "You know that technique is a forbidden form of attack against an opponent." The young man sighed deeply, and tried to contain the scowl on his face by hanging his head.

"You have been warned several times, and now, by ignoring our tradition, you have forfeited this match to your opponent. In addition, until you learn to respect our ways of combat, you are hereby barred from fighting amongst your fellow warriors. Now leave us."

The crowd booed as the young man was led from the ring. Kaladin watched in silence, remembering his own confrontation with the Council. At the same time he was struck by the possibility that another was searching for the truth. Thoughts of showing this young fighter and others like him what lay beyond the city's boundaries filled his head. But as he looked through the scornful crowd, he suddenly saw his parents and brother sitting in a box below the elder's section, and he was filled with a rush of love and compassion. Kaladin studied them closely for a moment and smiled. He had missed them terribly, but seeing them alive and well made him happy. Now he knew he could see them whenever he chose; it was simply a matter of traveling at the speed of thought.

Kaladin laughed to himself, knowing his insight could have been one of Tyban's lessons. *All perceived boundaries exist only in our minds*, he reminded himself. *There is no separation; only the illusion of separation.*

Kaladin mused on his revelation as the fights drew to a close. The crowd filed out into the city streets, leaving him alone in the dark giant that was the Arena.

As he closed his eyes and let his thoughts trail off, the silence of the empty Arena was replaced by the soft sound of gentle ocean waves. Kaladin looked around to find himself sitting on the ridge where he had begun meditating an hour before. Surprisingly, perched on his right knee was his familiar companion, the little butterfly. It flapped its wings ever so slowly, to the rhythm of Kaladin's breathing. Then, in the next instant, it fluttered off over the edge of the embankment and up to the sky above. Energized and excited by his experience, Kaladin smiled and leaned back against a tree as the moon began to rise over the sparkling water below.

CHAPTER 21

Tyban, it was amazing!" Kaladin exclaimed, recounting his experience of the night before. The pair had just finished practicing an ancient sword pattern in open field on the edge of the settlement.

"I didn't make any effort, yet I was there, in the blink of an eye. I never dreamed such things were possible."

"That and much more, Kaladin," Tyban said with a smile.

"Even more? It's hard to imagine," Kaladin said.

"Mental projection grows easier as you become more familiar with the new territory you are exploring. Your imagination is limited only by the boundaries of your experience. As you continue to experience more and more, your imagination reaches beyond the horizon of your perception, pulling you forward. Indeed, even the most advanced amongst us has only begun to glimpse what lies beyond this layer of reality."

"How can it be, though? How can any of it be?"

"It *can* be however it wants to be. The reason sudden insights and jumps forward can seem so difficult to understand is only due to our limited perception. We've chopped the world up into tiny pieces that we call 'life,' and anything outside 'life' that doesn't fit those particular rules seems strange, even frightening. But, to see it from a limitless point of view, nothing is beyond the realm of possibility. To have a desire instantly fulfilled in the silence between thoughts, to you, seems unbelievable, but from an unlimited point of view it's just the most efficient way to get things done."

"I'm not sure I understand what you mean," Kaladin said.

"The shortest distance between two points, Kaladin, is *simplicity*. Nature, *your nature*, is not complex. It searches for the quickest and most effortless means of fulfilling any desire. And the greater the unnecessary clutter of boundaries, limitations and resistance you carry with you, the more difficult life becomes. But as you're beginning to discover, as those restrictions fall away, less effort is required. Remember the battle with your Shadow?"

"Yes." Kaladin reflected on how overcoming his dark side ultimately came about not through struggle, but by simply shifting his perspective.

"I'm still amazed, though."

"Good," Tyban replied. "Don't loose that. When you are able to see each new day as a miracle, life itself becomes pure magic."

"What do you mean?" Kaladin asked.

"See for yourself. We all make our own answers. No one else has yours. What does your heart tell you?"

Kaladin let his mind go blank for a moment. He considered all he had learned and the excitement it had brought him. The changes he had seen, the miracles of his own expanding awareness. The joy he felt regarding his own process was incredible, but he knew there was something more, something pulling him onward.

Then he remembered the young man driven from the Arena the night before. He remembered wanting to reach out to him and others who might be ready to learn what he knew. If his own evolution had brought such happiness, how much more could he feel by helping others find their truth?

"My heart tells me to teach, Tyban, like you. I can feel it now. It's what I have to do."

Tyban smiled. "Well spoken, Kaladin. If you truly wish to keep growing, there is no better path. Indeed, teaching may be the highest expression of any art."

"But am I ready?"

"Once again, that is for you to answer. However, know that to be able to teach you need only the willingness to teach what *you* have learned. Believe that you can teach and you *can*. Begin with what you know and express it in your own unique way. Your ability to express yourself will grow as you do, and the rest will take care of itself spontaneously."

Kaladin was excited. "Yes, I am ready. I'm ready...*now!*"

"Then what are you waiting for? Your path is calling," Tyban said with a grin.

"You know where I must go, Tyban," Kaladin said reluctantly.

"I do. But remember, the journey isn't about seeing new landscapes, it's about seeing with new eyes."

"I will," Kaladin replied.

Pausing momentarily, Kaladin took a slow look around at the beauty surrounding them. Through the trees he could see the open valley and spire of the Grand Temple. Beyond the valley a crimson sun was hovering over the lake's surface.

"I will miss this place and *especially* you," Kaladin sighed. "But I have the feeling we'll see each other again."

"Of course, because whatever you imagine, you can create in this world. You'll never be far, and if ever you need to talk, I'll be here."

Tyban raised his hands, folded them in front of his chest and bowed his head slightly.

Kaladin returned the gesture with a smile and closed his eyes. He emptied his mind of all thought and slipped into silence as he had done the night before. Then, as he brought his attention to thoughts of Thelius, his body faded until only emptiness filled the spot where he had been standing.

EPILOGUE

The streets of Thelius were deserted. The evening fights had long been over and everyone had gone home for the night. Only Orin Baluk remained. He was sulking on a bench in a courtyard not far from the Arena. Since his humiliation several nights before, the courtyard had become a place of refuge during the fights, which he could no longer attend. The moonlight covered him in a blue glow as he remembered his expulsion from the fight in painstaking detail.

"Why can't they see it?" he asked himself. "They call themselves warriors…hah! Warriors indeed! All they know are their rules and laws. If only I had…" He let his thoughts trail off. He realized that hoping to change the Council was a futile exercise. He knew he should be focusing on his training, but since the upset he had lost his motivation.

"Whatever I learn, they'll just tell me I can't do it. What's the point?" he thought out loud. "However I might progress, the Council just tightens their grip until I have no choice but to live their lie."

In his frustration Orin didn't hear the sounds of footsteps approaching. When he realized he was no longer alone, he looked up to see four young men glaring down at him.

"Well, look who we have here," the leader said. "A little rebel sulking in the corner."

Orin had seen these men before. The sons of the high elders, they were the new guard of the city's heritage. He had watched them fight with almost fanatical devotion to the city's warrior tradition. They were very good, but Orin knew they lacked his vision. He didn't know what they wanted, but he was sure it wasn't good.

"So this is where he's been hiding," one of the others said. "Afraid to show your face?"

Orin bit his tongue. He struggled to keep his temper under control. He wanted to show them that he wasn't afraid, but he knew he was outnumbered. Lacking any rules, street fights could often be as bloody as, if not worse than, the formal matches in the ring. "No, I just wanted to be alone," Orin muttered.

"Well, you're not alone now, and I think we're going to have to show you what we do to traitors like you," the leader replied.

"I'm no traitor," Orin retorted. "I just wanted to..."

"*We* think you're a traitor, and that's all that matters." The men started to close in on Orin, who jumped to his feet and began backing toward a wall.

"Look," Orin reasoned. "I'm not worth it. I don't want to fight."

"Now you're a coward as well as a traitor?" one of the men sputtered. They were almost on top of him now, and Orin knew he'd have to act fast to avoid being *seriously* hurt.

The leader of the group crouched into a stance, ready to make the first move, when suddenly his attention was drawn by a momentary flicker of light from the corner of the courtyard. "Who's there?" he shouted. Orin turned slightly to look toward the corner as well. All he could see was a person seated on the edge of a stone bench, his body covered by a dark, hooded cloak.

"No one to concern yourself over," a soft voice replied. "I was just passing through and thought I'd rest here after watching the fights. I hope I'm not disturbing you."

There was a long pause. "No…um…no," the leader replied. "We were just having a…discussion." Orin peered at the figure, but couldn't make out any features he could recognize. Oddly, Orin knew he had been alone in the courtyard before.

"Well, don't let me disturb you." The stranger rose and walked toward the street, stopping briefly between Orin and his would-be antagonists. He looked deeply into the eyes of the gang's leader. After a brief pause, he turned to look at Orin. "I wish you all a pleasant evening," he said smiling, and continued out into the street.

The four men paused awkwardly for a moment before managing to stammer, "And…to you."

The courtyard seemed noticeably brighter as the figure walked toward the gate, leaving Orin and his opponents in silence.

The four men looked at each other and then at Orin.

The leader broke the silence. "I guess this will wait for another time." He turned to his friends. "Let's go." The four men turned and walked toward the street, the last one pausing to look back briefly at Orin in the empty courtyard.

Orin sighed deeply and leaned up against the wall. How had he avoided almost certain death just now? Who was that stranger and why did he seem oddly familiar? As he began to relax, his curiosity got the better of him and Orin ventured out into the night to look around.

Stepping out into the street, Orin could see the cloaked figure rounding a corner near the city square. He mustered up his courage and ran toward the stranger, hoping to catch a better look.

When he was just a few feet away, the stranger quietly turned and said, "Hello, Orin."

"Uh, hello," replied Orin, startled to be called by name.

"How do you know my name?" Orin asked.

"Oh, the same way my teacher knew mine. It's a little difficult to explain." The stranger removed his hood to reveal a peaceful, comforting face.

"But who are you?" Orin insisted.

"I'm a friend, Orin, a friend who can show you another side of yourself and the ways of combat."

Orin's eyes widened.

"If you're interested, why not take a walk with me? I have a story I'd like to tell you."

"A story?" Orin asked.

"Yes." The stranger paused for a moment and smiled. "It's the story of a warrior; a warrior like you."

End

Adam Brady has been a student of self-development and conscious evolution for over 25 years. Holding a B.A. from Westminster College in New Wilmington PA, Adam has been certified by Chopra Center University in Carlsbad, California as a Vedic Master Educator and is qualified to teach Primordial Sound Meditation, Perfect Health: Ayurvedic Lifestyle, and the Seven Spiritual Laws of Yoga. Adam is a certified Jeet Kune Do and Action Strength Functional Fitness instructor and holds a 1st degree Black Belt in To Shin Do. Adam is dedicated to helping people transform their lives through a consciousness-based approach to living and regularly teaches in the Orlando, FL area. For additional information on Adam visit www.revisedreality.com

Printed in Great Britain
by Amazon